New Fiction

MYSTERIOUS MEETINGS

Edited by

Sarah Marshall

First published in Great Britain in 2005 by
NEW FICTION
Remus House,
Coltsfoot Drive,
Peterborough, PE2 9JX
Telephone (01733) 898101
Fax (01733) 313524

SB ISBN 1 85929 134 1

FOREWORD

When 'New Fiction' ceased publishing there was much wailing and gnashing of teeth, the showcase for the short story had offered an opportunity for practitioners of the craft to demonstrate their talent.

Phoenix-like from the ashes, 'New Fiction' has risen with the sole purpose of bringing forth new and exciting short stories from new and exciting writers.

The art of the short story writer has been practised from ancient days, with many gifted writers producing small, but hauntingly memorable stories that linger in the imagination.

I believe this selection of stories will leave echoes in your mind for many days. Read on and enjoy the pleasure of that most perfect form of literature, the short story.

Parvus Est Bellus.

CONTENTS

THE VENGEANCE
Marcus Vorment

My mother was accused of witchcraft, she was burnt alive! I was forced to watch her death, I was promised that the fumes would kill her and she would suffer no pain from the flames. They lied!

I saw the flames lick her body while she screamed. I saw the spasms of energy in her body as it writhed to escape from the deadly fire, I saw her flesh recoil from the bitter agony that it caused, reeling from the pain in a last-ditch attempt in order to survive. I felt my mind twist and contort, borderlining on account of the ghastly sight that I beheld before me.

I felt disgusted at my own inadequacy and weakness to be able to help her. The pain of the knowledge of this was tearing my heart asunder. I was extremely sorrowful and upset to see her cry out for mercy, my soul felt as though it was in agony of death itself. My heart was burdened with unimaginable bitter anguish as I saw my own mother cry out like a baby. The whole thing was awful! How will I ever forget what happened that day? I can never forgive myself for not fighting those b*****ds to the death. I was just eight years old!

As I watched my mother die I was filled with pain; knowing her to be innocent, I had no cause for shame. She took one long agonising hour to die, her screams seemed to split the sky around me, until in her last moments they faded to whimpers as her will was broken and she accepted the inevitable. I looked upon the crowds there present, they seemed glad to witness her death. I looked at the puritan elders who had decided her fate, and, as an eight-year-old boy, I felt extremely confused. This God that they told me about who they say loves us, why would he want my mother killed in such a shocking manner?

The weeks that followed were almost as terrible, as I was forced to attend their schools and vow to believe in the vile doctrine that had my mother executed. Anyhow, I was still so in shock at the loss of my mother whom I loved I could not concentrate on anything that they were teaching me. Looking back, I can remember that the elders of the fellowship kept trying to remind me that it had been the Lord's will for my mother to be burnt at the stake. Perhaps they were trying to convince themselves?

As the weeks turned into months my sorrow began to be replaced by hatred until, one day, the headmaster of the school, Jeremy Wemyss, forced me to stand up in front of the class to tell the other pupils that it was righteous that my mother died.

After the school day had ended I was so grief-stricken by my own act of betrayal and cowardice that I took flight into the forest of the night, weeping bitterly, completely and utterly cut to the heart with anguish and remorse. Falling to my knees beside a little stream, I stared straight ahead into the forest, and the hatred within me was now so great that I uttered words that no eight-year-old boy could ever think of ...

'Oh spirit of vengeance and anger help me now in my weakness. My mother was not a witch, but as for me, do what you will, but give to me this one wish. That you transform my frail and cowardly form into the monster of vehemence, a sword of vengeance, an instrument of ever-raging fire!

If you can truly hear me, if you do exist, then destroy these monsters that ravaged my mother in fire and desecrated her unmarked grave!'

Exhausted, I fell on my face on the forest floor, not really understanding the words that I had just spoken, not understanding the source that gave me utterance. Hours passed and I was so weak that even rabbits and squirrels had no fear of me and came right up to my face, sniffing as thought to investigate.

The elders of the village discovered me and dragged me away violently. They caged me up that night like a wild animal instead of leaving me in my much-hated puritanical new adoptive home.

The next day I was severely beaten with rods in front of the whole school until I felt the blood run down my back. Despite the pain, I could sense the power of my hatred grow in strength with each stroke, vowing in my own mind that someday when I was old enough I would kill every last one of these b*****rds, including the villagers that had been present at my mother's death.

The years passed by and in the meantime, I had learnt to pretend. They thought that they had made a disciple out of me, but instead I watched them all intently, studying every flaw, every weakness, keeping at all times in my mind's eye my moment of vengeance, which would one day surely come. By the age of eighteen I had almost forgotten my prayer to the spirit of vengeance, until one night I was visited by strange dark shadows in the corner of my room, accompanied by a vile odour that I knew now to be the smell of deepest rage and evil.

At first I recoiled from the powers of darkness in great fear and trembling, but after that moment my state of mind began to sink to the lowest level of human depravity and disgust I could ever have imagined. I continued to be filled with a gruesome dark loathing of myself and humanity. I no longer felt human, I kept asking myself, *Am I evil?*

From now on my heart of vengeance was an ever-raging fire! I began to bury dogs alive in a makeshift cemetery of my own. This was so that when the time was right, their spirits would aid me upon the eve of my declaration of war. I stole the dogs from many different villages so as not to raise suspicion against myself, and, eventually, I also buried a horse.

On the night that I buried the horse I witnessed a supernatural presence of a very different kind. Was this God? It did not speak, but I felt as though this presence was trying to tell me that there was still yet time to change my mind, and that the people that had killed my mother had followed a God that they themselves had created, and not the supernatural presence that was with me this night. The opportunity lay before me to be at peace at last, and the feeling that this presence gave was one of indescribable beauty.

This was a shock to me, but after having given this some thought, I decided that I wanted to continue with my path of vengeance, to destroy those who had murdered my mother. No, I did not desire to forgive the murderers of my mother. Instead I wanted to spend each day dwelling upon vile and perverse ways of imposing intense suffering upon them all. From this moment on I could not recognise anything of humanity left in me, just a malignant other that was obsessed with the annihilation of the village.

Am I evil? Yes I am!

One evening in the late summer, the soldiers had left the village undefended as they were on a mission to capture some highway bandits, and, brandishing a sword that I had hidden for this moment, I smote the village with a great and dreadful anger!

Upon finding Jeremy Wemyss, the headmaster of the school, I looked down on his now old and sickly form as I burst into his home. He begged for mercy, instead I gave pain! I pushed him head first into the hearth of his own fire, and held him there while he screamed to his last breath.

I also found the b*****d puritan who had sentenced my mother to death. He held out his hand to plead and I struck it with my sword between the two centre fingers and it split his arm down to the elbow. I then cut out his bowels while he was still alive and burnt them in front of his very face. Villagers came to the rescue but I felt as though I was possessed by a supernatural strength that knew no bounds. I must have severed at least twenty heads in the first thirty seconds, and then I saw something that surprised and shook me to the core!

The dark shadows that I had seen only by night seemed to emerge and assist me by causing the buildings to spontaneously burst into flames. Everywhere the villagers tried to flee in terror and wherever I met them they fell by the edge of the sword.

As I stood in the village square a horse came charging towards me. It was featureless and completely black with no eyes, more like a shadow. I mounted the horse and immediately was compelled to charge headlong into a towering wall of fire that had sprung up.

I entered the inferno as a man.

I came out the other side in spirit form only.

The dogs that I had buried now surrounded the village on all sides. Their eyes were red and supernatural, ablaze with fury and unfathomable evil. I was now a different person in a sense. I had my chance to stop, but now it was too late, my mind was consumed by a terrible passion to administer evil. I no longer needed a sword, as the very sight of me, the phantom horse and the devil dogs struck so much terror into the victims that they dropped dead from heart attack where they stood.

Some of the villagers had escaped; at this point I vowed that I would even hunt down their descendants through the centuries to come, carrying out my vengeance, and indeed my own eternal doom until all of my mother's tormentors were destroyed.

Devonshire, England, present day.

DCI Torrance arrived at the scene of death at 07.43 hours. The weather was typically murky for an autumn day on Dartmoor. Sergeant Hynes revealed to him the bodies of the two backpackers.

'Sir, there are no signs of foul play but look at the eyes! What was going through their minds just before their deaths? God only knows.'

The eyes of the two backpackers had almost bleached to pure white, the pupils had shrunk to the size of pinheads. Their faces had been fixed in a death mask of pure terror.

'They were not murdered by any human assailant, Hynes,' Torrance replied.

'Sir, what are you suggesting?'

'I was on these very moors with DCI Cronin in 1987 looking for an escaped convict from the prison one night when we saw them, the headless horseman and his pack of spectral hounds. This is where they come, driving people to their deaths over the edge of Dewerstone Rock.'

'What happened, Sir?'

'Cronin threw himself over this edge, just as these two have done, but I managed to hold out and lay on the ground. Then it happened. The apparition lay directly on top of me, its face pressed against mine! The only thing was, it had no face, no head, no body, no hands, nothing, just the clothing that it was in. Yet though its face was not visible to me, it was the most terrifying face I have ever seen.

The hospital told me that I continued to scream for the next three days, though I cannot remember it.'

Sergeant Hynes took a gulp of air. Something in Torrance's tone told him that his experience was for real, and, because of the older policeman's seniority, Hynes dared not doubt him.

UNKNOWN, UNSEEN
Ann Odger

The foetid smell filled the boy's nostrils as he passed the gibbet, where the bloated remains of the rotting corpse swung to and fro in the wind. He felt sick and afraid, desperately trying not to look sideways as he ran down the lane, the cold striking through his ragged clothes. His short trousers had been patched so many times that there was very little left of the original cloth. His jacket was a hand-me-down from his older brother and too thin to keep the biting cold wind out. Both his shoes had holes in the soles and he winced as another small stone found its way under his foot.

Suddenly the moon was hidden by cloud and the boy ran faster, wishing home was near. He was thinking of the meagre supper that his mother would have ready for him and hoped that there would be enough warmth from the fire that smoked and smelt of the peat.

He stopped abruptly, his heart beating faster, he felt as if someone or something was nearby. He glanced fearfully either side of the trees and bushes rustling with the wind, but could see nothing while it was so dark. He shivered, but it wasn't just with the cold this time. He desperately wanted to run on but his feet seemed glued to the ground.

Without any warning, his body was crushed and drained of blood before he could scream and his remains tossed into the bushes. The lane looked just as before, no sign of life at all, just the dark and the sound of the wind.

In the cottage, the boy's mother was anxiously waiting for her son's return. It was well past the time that he should have been home and she began to imagine all sorts of things. 'Danny, please go and have a look outside to see if he is coming.' Her eldest son went out of the door and down to the gate, but there was no one to see. He shook his head as he re-entered the kitchen and his mother heaved a sigh. 'It's too dark to go searching tonight, if he's not home soon, I shall go to bed and we will have to look for him in the morning.'

Life to her had been one long struggle since her husband had gone to prison, and she was too proud to ask for help, although there were those in the village who still spoke to her. She took the candle from the table and made her way up the creaking stairs, leaving Danny to finish his supper.

The next morning after she had found her son's bed still empty, she called Danny to come down quickly. 'You will have to go and see if you can find him now it is light. I have this feeling that something terrible has happened to him.'

Danny hurried down the path and into the lane, looking from side to side as he went. He came across the remains of his brother's body before long and, after throwing up, he ran as fast as he could back home.

'Mother, you will have to be very brave and stay here while I go to the village for help. I have found Jack, but you must not go out there yourself. Please do as I ask.'

With that, he turned and went out again, running into the village to find the Chief Elder. He knocked loudly until the Elder came to the door. 'What is it boy?' He was not pleased to be roused so early.

'Oh, Mister Thomas, can you come with me? My brother has been horribly murdered and I don't know what to do.'

'Wait here while I get my coat on then,' and he went back inside but reappeared straight away. 'Right then, you had better take me to him.' They made their way back to the spot, but Danny could not bear to look again.

'Good grief, I have never seen anything like it. I shall have to report this to the authorities. Go back home now and I will take care of things. Give my condolences to your mother.'

Some time later, two of the village women came to see his mother to offer help with the funeral. 'What a terrible thing to happen to your boy, Mrs Burton. I know how you must feel. I lost a son last year.' Danny's mother thanked them for their kindness and in due course after the authorities had examined the body, they allowed Jack to be buried.

A few weeks later, a woman from the village was tidying weeds in the graveyard. She noticed it seemed eerily quiet, not even the birds were singing, but went on with what she was doing.

Without warning, her body became distorted and withered as it was drained of its life blood and hurled across the graves.

She was later found by her brother and once again the Elder was called upon. By the time the authorities had been notified and examined the latest corpse, the whole village was fearful and wondering what was out there that could be inflicting such terrible injuries.

People began staying in of a night and never went out alone in the day if they could help it. It was ten miles to the nearest town where the authorities, such as they were, kept a scant record of all events. Someone was sent to the village to make enquiries about the deaths, but the villagers could not shed any light on either of them.

A month went by and Mrs Johns was hanging out the washing in her garden. 'Joseph,' she called to her son, 'can you bring out the basket by the back door for me please? Then you can go and play on the green with Jimmy. Don't wander off either.' She was humming to herself as she bent down for the pegs. Suddenly she was violently pushed to the ground and screamed as great chunks of her flesh were gouged out by some unseen force, all trace of her blood removed and her remains tossed to one side.

Her husband had rushed out when she had screamed and had stood transfixed. He had seen what had happened to her, but there had been nothing there. For a while he became demented, not wanting to believe what had happened. Then he made his way to the Elder's house and gave a garbled account of what he had seen. The Elder was at a loss as to what to do next. How could he deal with something that was invisible?

He tried his best to calm the villagers, but it was difficult when he was frightened himself. Nothing made any sense, although he did wonder if some large animal was responsible and perhaps the man had imagined what he had found because of his grief.

He summoned the villagers to a meeting in the local farmer's barn and they drew comfort from being together for that short time. 'I know you expect me to help you by solving the mystery and putting your minds at rest, but I have to admit that I don't have any answers now.' He sighed as he spoke, feeling utterly helpless. They all tried to speak at once, making suggestions, none of which were practical, but at least they were united in their determination to find the culprit. 'All I can tell you to do, is stay together as much as possible and don't go to places that aren't used much.' They made their way home without another word, there wasn't anything they could say that would make the problem go away.

Three months passed and they all began to relax, hoping that whatever had caused the deaths had gone away from the area.

Three farm workers were out in the field repairing a fence, when one by one they were seized and their heads ripped off. This time the bodies were left on the ground without being thrown, but the blood had been sucked from them as before.

The Elder had reported the deaths as usual, but nothing seemed to be happening as far as the authorities were concerned. It was as if they weren't interested, or perhaps too afraid for themselves. Either way, the Elder felt as if the whole nightmare was his responsibility. He called another meeting in the barn to which everyone turned up, most of them had some sort of stick, pitchfork, or weapon with them. It gave them a small sense of protection anyway. It was beginning to get dark, which the Elder was sorry for, but he had had other important matters to attend to that day.

'I know you are all frightened about what has been happening, with good reason, but we are up against something we know nothing about. It seems to be invisible, which makes it impossible to fight against. I am aware that some of you are thinking of the occult and black magic, but there must be another reason for it.'

As he finished speaking, there was a brilliant light outside and they rushed to see what was causing it. High up in the sky, there had appeared a strange shaped object, a beam of light was shining straight down to the ground and, just for an instant, there was an inhuman shriek, something seemed to be drawn upwards in the beam. The light disappeared and the object just vanished. The people stood there, looking at one another in complete silence. Without a word, they all left the barn and returned to their homes.

The following day, the Elder reported the odd phenomena to the authorities, who looked at him as if he must have been drinking, but after he had left, a final entry was made in the record. 'Unknown, unseen', was all it said and the case was closed. No further deaths other than through natural causes happened and village life returned to normal.

BETTER DEAD
P T Rodge

Tomkin grinned, jigging around in a tight little circle like some crouched hobgoblin as he carefully unscrewed the top of the canister. They were all fools. They knew nothing with all their stupid theories about Dracula and vampires. Dracula was just a story, a fiction based on a myth.

Then there were those who said that the myth was based on the story of Vlad the Impaler. Vlad was no vampire, not in the true sense of the word. He may have been a Dracule, a physical one, but the myth did not belong to him. The myth was more.

It had taken Tomkin years to track down the reality behind the ancient folk tales and to discount all the diversions created by so called academics in their search for the truth. The truth was here. The truth was now, and he was going to reawaken it.

Tomkin carefully emptied the contents of the stoneware pot onto the small pile of earth that he had built up into a mound with a hollowed centre so that it looked like a small volcano. Marked on the floor around this mound was a circle made from a mixture of salt, chalk, dust and ground frankincense. It was a mixture he had carefully made according to the proportions described in the old scroll that now lay unrolled on the table. He referred to the scroll again giggling with excitement. He could imagine what would happen if he got this wrong, but he wasn't going to do that.

'Light the candles,' he said to himself picking up the matches. 'From one flame, west, east, south, north.' He used a match to light a taper. 'No skimping now,' he told himself glancing at the scroll to remind himself of the words to be said as each was lit, although he had no need. These words had long been committed to memory.

'Ha!' It was done and all in time for now was the dark of the moon. Only one thing was left to do. Tomkin looked at his watch, then around the darkened ruin and then back to the flagstone floor checking, thinking, looking for anything that he had missed but he had rehearsed it, practised it. Only the final piece of the jigsaw needed to be fitted into place.

The girl wanted to scream but could only manage a whimper as the chain that held the door shut was unwound and the door creaked open.

His eyes were wide, his teeth showed a grin and he was naked, naked and aroused. Christ, she didn't want to be raped but she had been expecting it ever since he had beaten her and ripped her clothes off. She had expected it then but he had locked her in, leaving her huddled and naked.

It had seemed like fun at first. He had picked her up in the club, bought her a drink, danced. He seemed nice and she was tempted. Not that she made a habit of sleeping with a boy on the first date, but Tommy seemed nice and kept buying her drinks and she had begun to feel a bit giggly.

Perhaps he had slipped something into her drink. Perhaps that was it. He slipped something into her drink to make her all squiffy and then she had agreed to leave with him. She didn't like this place though. If he had taken her to his flat it would have been alright. She would have let him then and just put it down to experience. She didn't like this place. It was dark and spooky, but when she had started to complain, he had hit her. Then again, and again, and tore her dress and pants and bra.

She shivered, curling into a ball, arms wrapped around her body shielding herself from him, expecting him to leap on her. Perhaps if she let him he wouldn't kill her. It was her only hope.

'Why did you hit me?'

'You said you wanted to go home.'

'This place scared me. I know what you want. I don't mind really, in fact I quite fancy you. It's just this place scared me.'

Tomkin grinned. It would be easier if she thought that. The timing had to be right and if she struggled he might have to hit her again and then drag her or carry her. 'OK then.' He held out his hand.

She trembled, then reached out nervously, her fingers touching his. She would have to stand and she couldn't hide her nakedness if she did, but if she didn't, he would force her. She stood gritting her teeth, fighting back the humiliation, and followed as he led her out of the small dungeon-like room into what looked like some huge cellar with vaulted ceilings.

The candlelight grew brighter as they approached and she tried to make sense of the circle and the markings on the floor as he guided her to step inside the markings. 'Kneel,' he said.

She shivered. Alright, if this was what he wanted, then she would do it. At least if she could satisfy him this way he might not actually rape her. She knelt but he moved around behind her, stroking her hair and gathering it as if in a ponytail. His hands ran through her hair and over her shoulders and she looked down at the small pile of earth topped with what looked like black crusty ash. 'What are you going to do with me?'

He was chanting, mumbling some strange unfathomable litany and suddenly she felt afraid. Perhaps she had it wrong. Perhaps he didn't plan to rape her at all.

The razor-sharp blade flashed silver in the candlelight. He held her hair tight pulling it back stretching the wide gash he had slashed across her neck. Blood fountained out splattering around in huge droplets while more flowed down over and between her naked breasts onto his carefully crafted mound which steamed and crackled as if suddenly empowered; as if about to erupt.

Tomkin held her body, letting it drain, then stepped back throwing it onto the blood-splattered stone before carefully stepping outside of the circle. Now he must prepare for the next stage.

The mound grew slowly, its form changing into something resembling a translucent jelly which then grew larger, with tendrils reaching the girl's body. These tendrils closed in on the puddled blood sucking at it like straws. Other splatters and droplets were sought out, nothing was wasted. The blob grew, taking more form, more shape, solidifying as it stretched upwards until it stood.

'Welcome back, Master.'

The Master looked around. 'You have done this?'

Tomkin grinned. 'All my own work. Finding you, the words, the spell, the girl.'

The Master looked down at the dead body at his feet and then at the circle which he gingerly tested with the toe of his black pointed boot. 'And yet you keep me prisoner.'

'Oh no, Master. I have no desire to keep you prisoner. I brought you back. I brought you back so that you could be free, so that you could fly just like it was in the old days.'

'Why?'

Tomkin looked puzzled at the question. 'Because you are the Master. Because you have a right to live.'

'Live?'

'Exist then. Exist. You have a right to exist.'

'And what of you? What is it you desire for what you have done?'

This was it. He was being asked the desire that had filled his mind for years and now he would receive his reward. 'I want to serve you, Master, and I want people to look up to me and fear me because I serve the Master. After all, I brought you back so it's only fair.'

'The Master snarled angrily. 'Fair! What do you know of what's fair? You took the life of this girl, was that fair?'

'But I did it for you, Master. I did it because I want to serve you.'

'If the Master wants a servant then it is for the Master to choose the servant, not for the servant to choose the Master.'

'But you were dead.'

'Yes! I was dead. I was at rest, at peace and yet now I am still not alive. I am undead, unable to seek death, to seek peace, though I can desire them both with a desire stronger than any you know or have dreamed of. Now I am here and I have other desires, the desire to feed and exist, and these desires grow stronger. I am torn between the two. The desire to exist and the desire to not exist and it is you, you who have resurrected this curse upon my soul.'

Tomkin fell back from the Master's rage, reaching for the implements he had secreted away in his bag. 'I'm sorry! I can send you back.'

'Do you think I can let you?' the Master spat out snarling and for the first time showing his curved yellow fangs. 'I'll feed on your blood first.'

Tomkin felt the glass bottle between his fingers, yanked at the stopper and threw it. The water sizzled on the Master's flesh but did little else other than increase his rage. His arms raised, clawed hands outstretched. He would taste blood, fresh blood, Tomkin's blood.

Tomkin charged, aiming the wooden stake for where legend said it had to go.

The stake struck home. The Master screamed. Clawed fingers raked at Tomkin's back. Blood sprayed across his body. Lighted candles were kicked away. One rolled next to the old scroll that had fallen from the table and it flared into a bright greenish light. Tomkin screamed as his flesh tore open. The Master screamed, desire to exist, desire to die mingled as the point of the stake bit home, splitting his undead, unbeating heart and once again flesh turned to dust.

A sudden flash of torchlight lit the scene. 'Bloody hell.' It moved across the flagstones lighting on the girl, her head almost severed by the knife that lay at her side.

'Bloody hell.'

One of the policemen turned to puke. The other grabbed Tomkin, forcing his arms behind his back, snapping on handcuffs.

'I don't know how the hell you're going to explain your way out of this lot my lad,' he snarled.

Tomkin looked. He didn't know either.

BRAMPTON HALL
Rita Eyrl

A scream reverberated throughout the hall. *Had that come from me?* apparently so, judging by the reaction of the other two. As they both ran towards me asking 'Are you alright? What happened?'

With Julie thrusting a glass of water into my hands and Yvette grabbing a tea towel and frantically fanning me, I tried to drink, but the glass clanked against my teeth and my hands shook so much that I spilt most of the water.

'I said we were mad to hold a séance here,' said Yvette, 'I know Brampton Hall is a private house now, but it was once a hospice, so we were bound to conjure something up.'

'Oh don't be such a wimp, you know it's a good opportunity to have some fun while the owners are away. Anyhow, nothing happened at the séance last night,' Julie pointed out, 'so why did you scream Sarah?'

'I saw something horrible, really vile,' and thinking of the image I'd seen I began to feel faint and I started to retch.

It was an hour and two strong cups of coffee later before we all slid back into our everyday work routines. I avoided the area where I'd seen the apparition, but I knew eventually I would have to confront my fears. Unfortunately that day came sooner than I'd expected.

'Sarah, would you fetch the polisher and work in the library?' asked Yvette, 'I'd do it myself but I've been asked to change the bed linen this morning.'

'Where's Julie?' I asked, hoping she would be available.

'I'm afraid she's busy in the kitchen, sorry,' said Yvette.

Both Julie and Yvette had worked in the library, they had seen nothing unusual, and since that day I had almost convinced myself I'd found a logical explanation. It is because I'm an avid reader of horror stories that I somehow must have superimposed one of those terrifying images onto the face of a bust. Even so, it was with trepidation that I began working in the library.

This time I didn't scream, I just stood rooted to the spot. On this occasion a young woman gradually materialised. She was wearing a long black dress and was holding a glass of wine while standing next to a plinth, which was host to a bust of a Roman emperor.

I felt sick as once again blood started to ooze from the bust's mouth and trickle down its chin, plopping into the woman's glass, turning her white wine red. Slowly the bust's mouth opened revealing the fact he was devouring what appeared to be a human embryo.

A month later we were enjoying ourselves at a charity ball, held at Brampton Hall. The band began playing 'I must remember this'.

Yvette swaying slightly to the music said, 'Isn't it romantic?'

'Yes it is, but I must nip upstairs to the bathroom,' I said. I was humming the hypnotic tune as I made my way upstairs, nearing the top I sang softly, 'The fundamental things apply.'

'As time goes by,' sang someone, finishing the song for me. The singing seemed to be coming from a bedroom, and as I approached the door it slowly opened. Cautiously I stepped inside. No one was there. *Bang!* I nearly jumped out of my skin, I turned sharply towards the noise. Rooks were suddenly attacking the bedroom window outside. The noise of the rooks pecking at the window grew louder and increasingly menacing as more added to their number. I ran towards the door, my heart pounding, but the door slammed shut, cutting off my retreat.

'As time goes by,' someone sang again.

Fearfully I looked round and saw my reflection in a full length mirror nearby. I was startled to see my ballgown was now black in the mirror, instead of the red gown I had been wearing.

I stepped back in alarm as the reflection moved on its own. It raised its arm, outstretched its hand, then very slowly it began bending its fingers, the hand now looking like a claw. I felt pain in my chest, and when the fingers moved closer together the pain became intense. My heart felt as if it was in a vice, and I trembled with pain and fear. 'Why are you doing this?' I groaned sinking to my knees.

'When the bust's mouth opened, it was me you saw. My mother was carrying two babies. You are my twin, but for one to survive, the other had to die,' she retorted.

I was astounded. I was looking at my identical twin sister, and it was as if I was seeing myself. Then I saw that she moved her fingers again and now they were almost touching. My whole being filled with terror. I felt so ill. 'Please stop,' I begged.

'I had a right to live,' she continued, 'and now I'm claiming that right.' Her fingers touched and I gasped for air, the pain was excruciating, at the same time I felt as if I was being pulled towards the mirror by some magnetic force.

As my sister and I passed each other through the mirror, our ballgowns changed colour, hers to red, mine to black. She now had colour, life, my life. I was left without colour, only blackness and a void.

COPPER
Marty Grief

Chris flopped into his bed with a satisfied groan; his first night in his new flat, he mused, but oh God did he ache. He'd been moving furniture and lugging boxes around all day, his muscles were protesting over the abuse. He drifted into a much needed but fitful sleep.

When Chris awoke in the morning he gave an unsatisfied groan, he still ached. It was too early in the morning and he hadn't slept very well; too tired to sleep, his mum had used to say. He threw back the covers, stepped onto the cool bedroom floor and surveyed the mass of cardboard boxes that remained.

A few hours later, Chris was elbow deep in boxes. He felt a sharp, tearing pain as he snagged his hand on a box staple.

'S**t!' he cursed again as he ran to the door of his new flat. The door banged shut behind him.

That night, Chris was trying to sleep but his hand throbbed, it had only required a couple of stitches and he'd been given some pain killers, but it still hurt like crazy. Chris had resigned himself to getting little sleep, but a few minutes later he was sound asleep.

The blood had dripped in such quantity that a wide pool had formed, it had been dripping for so long that the pool was cool and had started to congeal. The air was filled with a metallic scent, a sickly odour that was unmistakable and impossible to ignore. But it was the viscous, crimson pool that truly demanded attention, the sheer volume of blood commanded the senses and all thoughts ceased, bar one. One word remained in the mind: Murder.

Chris awoke with a start and wiped something red and sticky off of his face, he checked his injured hand, but the dressing revealed no fresh blood.

'Crazy arsed dream,' he muttered as he climbed out of bed. Chris made for the bathroom, stopped dead in his tracks as he saw the splats of blood he could have sworn that he'd wiped off the floor the night before. Must have missed some, he rationalised to himself as he went to get a damp cloth, although he could have definitely sworn he had wiped it all away.

Chris could see the blood dripping, he could hear it, smell it even. The congealing pool was there too; but Chris could not see where the blood was coming from. Something was being reflected in the blood, but it was blurred, moving too fast to be recognised. The metallic smell was so strong, so vivid, it could be tasted.

Chris awoke suddenly, retching; he ran to his bathroom and spat into the sink, his saliva tinted red, wiping his mouth with the back of his hand he removed a sticky residue; he spat again. Chris showered and dressed, he used and reused mouthwash a dozen times to try and get rid of the metallic taste. In the bedroom, Chris noticed a small reddish stain had appeared on the ceiling over his bed, a few red spots were dotted over his pillows, he pulled off his bedding and shoved it all in his laundry basket. Quickly jotting a note to the maintenance man, Chris then prepared for work; he slipped the note in the appropriate pigeon-hole on his way out.

Work was hard, it's difficult to concentrate when all you can think about is blood, blood, blood. Dripping blood, pools of it. Chris shook his head to clear his thoughts, to try and focus. Perhaps someone had been killed, murdered even, in the flat upstairs, the blood pooling, cooling, then dripping into his flat; Chris gagged and ran to the toilet, desperate to hold back vomit, to hold back the thought of the blood dripping into his mouth.

Chris was torn between the two visits he had to make, on one hand he wanted to chase up the maintenance man and be assured of a rational non-grisly explanation for the red fluid; on the other hand, checking on the welfare of a neighbour was a good thing to do. Also, the particular neighbour might just be the gorgeous brunette he'd seen on the stairway. The possibility of meeting the brunette won hands down. Chris knocked on the flat door, jiggled impatiently whilst waiting, then smiled a big smile when the gorgeous brunette opened the door.

'Hi there, sorry to trouble you, I live in the flat below.'

'Oh hi there,' she replied.

'Hi, erm, I've just moved in, so this probably sounds a bit strange, not knowing you at all; but is everything okay?'

'Huh?'

'Look, I've got all this red stuff leaking into my flat, my ceiling is all stained; did you spill something?'

'Oh, you've not spoken to Burt yet have you? He's had my floorboards up all afternoon. Talk to Burt, he'll explain.'

'Right, thanks then …'

The door clicked shut!

'My name's Chris, by the way, it was real nice meeting you, perhaps we could go out for a drink sometime …' Chris muttered to himself as he made his way back down the stairs. He knocked on Burt the maintenance man's door.

Chris did not get to speak to Burt, but did find a note from the errant maintenance man that had been slipped under his door. The note explained the source of the problem; copper water pipes had rusted and were leaking, the staining was due to the rust. The problem was too big for Burt and so a plumber had been called, but it would be at least a couple of days before work started. Chris resigned himself to more cleaning up for a few more days, but he moved his bed before sleeping.

The man was hanging upside down, blood streaming from dozens of shallow cuts all over his torso, the blood laid thickly on the floor, staining the floorboards a shiny crimson. The metallic tang filled the air, the pitter-patter of blood against the floor was deafening. The sickly scent grew thicker as the flowing blood filled the man's nose.

Chris gagged as he woke up, his nose completely blocked; he grabbed a tissue and cleared his airways of thick, red mucus.

'Oh s**t!' He looked up at his ceiling and blinked a couple of times in disbelief at a new red stain. 'S**t!'

Chris spent the day at home, cleaning, trying to shake off an unknown sense of despair, trying desperately to shake off an unwelcome sense of doom. He'd finished unpacking, but still felt unsettled. A plumber had apparently been, hummed and hah'd, and had come to agree with Burt, the ancient copper pipes did need replacing. It was going to be a big job, causing a lot of hassle, but anything was better than this constant mess. All day, Chris' thoughts were of blood and rusty copper pipes. The visceral thoughts finally drifted into crimson dreams as Chris fell asleep in his newly re-positioned bed.

The strong metallic scent filled the air, flecks of blood covered everything and still the pattering of hot, crimson blood hitting the cold, wooden floor pounded the hearing like thunder. The body swung, writing in agony and desperation, the face, so covered in blood it was unrecognisable, unfathomable and contorted in unbearable pain. The cooling lake of blood reflected the gruesome scene in blurry, scarlet form and it grew, spreading over the floor, growing, suffocating the wooden boards. Blood flowed into the man's nose, the air still heavy with the hot, metal odour, more blood filled the man's airways, choking him, drowning him in his own blood.

Pain and a sense of breathlessness awoke Chris, he lurched into his bathroom, hacking and wheezing over the sink until he had coughed up a thick, red phlegm. He sank to his knees, sobbing out of desperation and sheer exhaustion.

Chris was at some friends' house for dinner, Dave and Alison were excellent company, just what he needed, a respite from the metallic stench that was invading his flat. Alison had cooked up a treat as usual and Dave had chosen the perfect accompanying wine. Although the change of scenery and atmosphere was soothing, Chris could not help bemoaning the state of his flat.

'Bloody copper pipes, leaking all over the place, leaving big, ugly, red stains on my ceiling; filling my nose and mouth with red stuff, it's disgusting. All my bedding is ruined, I'm at my wits' end.'

'Red stuff?' Alison inquired.

'Yeah, the pipes have rusted and as they leak the water drips down all thick, greasy and red.' Dave had returned, a new bottle of wine in his hand. 'Can't be copper then,' he informed. 'Scientifically impossible.'

Alison rolled her eyes in a silent gesture of mock despair and muttered. 'High school science to the rescue once again.'

'All I'm saying is, copper doesn't rust, it oxidises, goes green. Whatever this 'red stuff' is, it has nothing to do with copper.' His lecture finished, Dave freshened Chris' glass with more wine.

Chris stumbled through the door to his flat, upset and more than a little drunk. *Copper doesn't rust, it oxidises, goes green.* He lurched into his bedroom, glared up at the angry, red stain over his bed.

'Why can't you be green? You should be green!' he shouted.

The smell of blood was heavy and putrid, the hot scarlet flush of blood streamed down the man's body. The blood covered the floor like a slick and slippery, crimson carpet. The body was swinging, swaying from the left to right; the warm, viscous, red fluid filled the man's nose, choking him and still the blood dripped onto the floor. Chris looked into the sticky puddle and could clearly see the reflection, it was his face, contorted in agony, swinging from left to right, choking, drowning in his own blood ...

Chris' funeral was over, he was officially gone. Internal bleeding was the doctor's verdict, but a reason for the bleeding, for the massive clot of blood that smothered Chris in his sleep was not forthcoming.

'It's my fault,' whispered Chris' grandad.

'No it's not Grandad, it's not anyone's fault,' Chris' sister assured.

'I should have warned him about that evil house.'

She shook her head. 'That's just an urban myth, I was teasing Chris about it before ... before he moved in.' Tears welled up in her eyes.

'Not every story whispered in the dark is a myth my girl. When I was a boy, a man died in that house, bled to death. No one ever knew if he was murdered, did it to himself or what, well if they did know, they never said. But us kids always told each other it was black magic. We knew and we stayed away from that house.'

'He died in Chris' flat?'

'No, he died in the top floor; but in the room below slept his wife. His blood leaked down, dripped into her mouth and drowned her, she drowned in blood. They always drown in blood.'

Three months later ...

Cheryl was busy unpacking, making her new flat her own. As she unwrapped her wine glasses she failed to notice one was cracked. The broken glass cut deep into her hand. Cheryl gasped in pain as blood filled the remnants of the glass and the palm of her hand. She watched in bemusement as the blood trickled through her fingers, dripping onto the floor; Cheryl watched in horror as the blood seemed to form the shape of a malevolent smile.

DARLING JANE
Shaun Whittington

It had been another exhausting nine hours for Jane Richards, and the thought of a hot shower and drinking the remaining bottle of white wine that she had in the fridge, made her eager left foot push harder on the accelerator pedal in her Renault.

The car was purring at a steady forty along the winding country roads and the murky evening, created by a concoction of the early winter evening and the black bellied clouds that hung portentously above, made her journey from the hospital, a surreal one. Whether it was the strain of her shift in the A&E department, or the fact she could only manage five hours' sleep before her shift, her mind was wayward and it was becoming harder to keep her concentration.

Civilisation was nowhere to be seen as soon as she passed Milford, and the road to her hometown in Rugeley was another four miles away, four miles of country road. She had made the same journey for years since becoming a nurse, but this time was different. This time she was drenched in paranoia, and she knew that Jeremy Watkins had been released into the cultured world a month ago. The thought of that psycho being anywhere in Rugeley made her thin frame shudder.

It only felt like yesterday since she started having untoward feelings towards her house, mainly her bedroom. At first she thought she was going crazy, but as the weeks went by, the more she noticed things weren't quite right in her room. She even tested her own sanity. She made her bed, making sure her quilt was perfectly straight, she then came back from work to discovered her quilt had been interfered with, it was as if someone laid or kneeled on the quilt. It became worse when she realised her underwear drawer had been tampered with, and even a favourite pair of her red lacy knickers had miraculously disappeared. The single life had suited the twenty-seven-year-old since splitting from her boyfriend nine months ago, but during her ordeal, she thought that a partner would have shared her anxiety, although her family were sympathetic she still had to go back to the flat and sleep there alone.

After informing the police, detectives watched her flat twenty-four hours a day. And it was on the third day that Jeremy was caught letting himself into Jane's flat ten minutes after she left for work. Detectives quietly walked into her accommodation and walked into Jane's bedroom and saw a pile of clothes thrown in the corner of her room, they were Jeremy's clothes. They opened the door further and caught the disturbed Watkins lying on Jane's bed, with his eyes closed wearing her underwear, and masturbating.

When she heard the information from the police she felt a mixture of relief and abhorrence, she was certain that there was something untoward in the flat, but never imagined that someone could be capable of such a despicable act. Jeremy had originally gone into her ground floor flat through the opened window, she had always left her window open when she was working, as her flat always smelt fusty if there was no air let into the place. According to what he told the police, when Jeremy entered Jane's apartment for the first time, he found one of Jane's house keys as he headed for the exit and was regularly letting himself into her house when she was going to work. He even wrote to her from his prison cell, which dumbfounded her.

How could the prison service allow a prisoner to do such a thing? She received an apology from the prison's director and she never received any further letters. She received five letters in all, but only opened two of them, she particularly remembered her first letter.

Darling Jane,

I am still angry that you have forced me to stay in this hellhole, although I can't blame you entirely. I can imagine you being upset about me watching you and sneaking into your house. Maybe I got my tactics wrong? But I won't give up on you that easily my darling. I can't wait to get out and see you again, to sleep in the same room as you would be a dream come true.

Love Jeremy.

After the first two letters she received, she started recognising the handwriting and decided not to open the remaining three, and it was then she decided to inform the police who then contacted the prison's director.

Preparing herself for his imminent release, she had acquired herself a two-year-old German Shepherd from the 'dog and cat home' that was situated a mile out of town. Her dog, Marvin, took a while to settle into her flat as his last owner spent most of his time beating the dog, and the cigar burns on its head could still be seen, but the moment Jane saw its wide cheerless eyes in the pound, she wanted him straight away. She loved him more than she had loved any man.

Her car had reached the Globe Island and she turned right onto the street Horsefair, she was nearly home. As soon as her headlights shone into her living room, she could see the mad dog pawing at the window, his ecstasy that his mistress had returned home always made her smile. She opened her front door and the German Shepherd pounced on her with delight and licked her face. She hugged her loveable canine.

'Hello my boy,' came Jane's excited salutation. She put her handbag down onto the kitchen table, quickly got dressed and picked up the red dog lead. Every time she had the lead in her hand, Marvin's excitement was tough to control. 'Ready for a walk my boy?' Marvin replied with a strident yap. 'Come on then.' Jane ruffled her dog's ears and kissed the top of his head and smiled. *Who needs a man?*

Half an hour had passed and the pair of them returned from their exercise session. Marvin was given a generous amount of jellied meat that included rabbit and duck. Jane decided just to have a cheese and ham sandwich as her hunger wasn't as bad as Marvin's, since devouring a steak pie at the canteen during her lunch break. As per usual, the winter evening was drawing in too quick for Jane's liking and it would only be a matter of hours before she would be back in her bed. It was eleven o'clock and with one hour remaining before her bedtime, she watched a programme she recorded the other night and sat on the couch in her sky-blue dressing grown, brushing her damp, short, brown hair after her quick shower and Marvin lay across the grey rug by the fireplace, facing the television also.

It was bedtime, Marvin had been let outside for a minute to do his business as Jane nervously stood by the door. Despite having the locks changed, her nerves were still shredded from the incidents that had happened before and her early nights were always down to the fact that it took her a long time to sleep because of her paranoia. Her nervous energy usually ended up exhausting her body and by one or two in the morning, she would be sleeping.

As soon as Marvin returned, she turned off the lights leaving the house in complete darkness, for weeks after the incident, she preferred to leave a hall light on, but it only made her paranoia worse, because of the unusual shadows it created. It also soothed her mind that Marvin would lie by the side of her bed, sometimes he would get up and walk to the living room and sleep on the rug, so Jane would leave her bedroom door open so that Marvin could wander in and out of the room without disturbing his owner.

Her eyes opened suddenly, after another hellish dream. Her bedroom was blacker than any night, ten seconds passed before she realised she was back in her room, she had only left mentally, but the heart was punching from inside her chest and the sweat trickled gently from her forehead down to her pencil-thin brows. She exhaled long and slow, she let her right arm drop down by the side of her bed as she felt for Marvin. Was he lying in the living room? She couldn't feel his fur coat, but felt the gentle licks from his tongue, she smiled.

'There you are boy,' she whispered sleepily, as the licks continued. Her rapid, shallow breathing had started to wane, her pulse had reduced its beats per minute and with her body now giving in to the tiredness once again, her eyes closed and sleep was reintroduced almost immediately.

Her palm almost smashed the alarm clock, as her hand hit the snooze button. Still lying under the duvet, she stretched her whole body. She reflected on her night and after her nightmare, she remembered opening her eyes on another two occasions. On the last occasion she thought she heard some kind of bump in the night, she didn't know whether she had left a window open or that Marvin had knocked something over, but she was that exhausted at the time, she couldn't care less.

She slipped out of the duvet and got to her feet, immediately reaching for her sky-blue dressing grown, desperate to cover her slim and cold body. She yawned again, bringing tears to her eyes and called out for Marvin. She walked along the hall whilst tying her dressing gown simultaneously. She hurried her steps towards the bathroom and put her right hand on her stomach where she was feeling the pain. She needed the toilet.

At first, Jane's eyes seemed to be cut off from her brain, there was a delay in her response and it took seconds to make her realise that she was looking at something horrific.

Marvin lay in the bath, his lifeless body was surrounded in his own blood, his throat was cut, his tongue hung helplessly out of his mouth and his fur was matted in his own blood. Her legs buckled slightly from the shock that hit her and she almost fell into the bathroom door as her head was hit by dizziness. She was unable to cry for her beloved pet and staggered out of the bathroom to go to her desk where the phone sat. Before she had chance to pick up the phone, she felt a slight breeze hit her exposed legs from the knee down. Her consternation was enhanced when she saw the evidence that her flat had been broken into, her front door was wide open and the glass was broken.

She went back to the desk and picked up the phone, her eyes were distracted by a piece of paper that sat next to the phone, she looked at the piece of paper before she had chance to dial the first digit. Tears, finally left her eyes, her temporal pulse hammered from inside her head and her breathing increased. Covered in a blanket of terror, she turned her head from side to side, hoping that she was alone in the flat. The message read:

Darling Jane

Although it was too dark to see you properly, I'm sure you looked beautiful last night as you slept. Unfortunately, Marvin was a little too overprotective for my liking, so he had to be dealt with. Why have a dog, when I can look after you?

PS Jeremy can lick hands too.

THE SECRET OF RYCROFT HALL
Graham France

Lisa cursed as the wheels of the little red van bounced from one waterlogged pothole to another. Rain lashed the windshield as cleaning equipment rattled in the back of the van. Lisa's companion, a surly seventeen-year-old called Hope, sat silently listening to loud rock music. Lisa doubted that she'd ever had more than four words out of the girl over the previous three times she'd worked with her. The earphones seemed to be a permanent feature, as did the Cleopatra style eye make-up, the black lipstick and the nose ring.

The van followed the muddy track and stopped at the huge, grey, stone gateposts. The wrought iron gates were open and the cobbled driveway extended all the way to the manor house. It was a huge building, set in sparse grounds and surrounded by a tall dry-stone wall.

Apparently the woman who owned it wanted them to clean the ground floor. Margie Smith, the usual cleaner for this job, had refused to go to the manor again and had since left the firm. Lisa drove along the driveway and parked the van close to the front door, unaware of the eyes watching the little van from behind discoloured net curtains as she rang the doorbell.

'Hello. My name is Estelle Rycroft.' Lisa was shocked. The woman who greeted her was no more than twenty-seven. She had waist length, straight, black hair, pale skin and striking hazel eyes. Her high, well-defined cheekbones accentuated her warm smile as she introduced herself. She wore a long, finely woven, purple silk dress which fell to her bare feet, with intricate floral designs on the neckline and sleeves. Lisa hated her instantly. 'I was wondering if you could work in the library, hallway and drawing room today?' As she spoke she gestured towards a room through an archway and one of the two closed doors leading from the hall. Lisa just nodded in reply. 'If you need anything, just give me a shout. I'll be in the kitchen.'

Lisa muttered, 'Hippy freak,' under her breath, as a soaking Hope came through the door with her arms clutching mops and plastic buckets.

The library was huge. She noticed that the bay window was made of old glass, each piece fixed into place with strips of lead. The windows at the sides of the bay were clear, but the flat central panel facing her was made of stained glass. The picture was of a white tree or plant, with flowers on it and little pink birds resting on the branches. The twisted white vine was planted in some kind of box that seemed to be giving off beams of light.

The rain on the glass sounded like fingers tapping on its surface. Lisa moved over to the desk. It looked hundreds of years old, with heavy brass fittings and as she quickly wiped a duster over it, she noticed a small animal skull resting on top of a sheaf of papers.

She then went over to the bookshelves. Why would anyone want so many books? Some were on Greek and Roman history. There were books on witchcraft, witch trials and magic. Other books were written in some funny language she couldn't read. All rubbish!

She checked her watch. Time the moved on to the hallway. She nudged Hope, 'Time we started on the hall.' The girl followed her out the library without a word, head bowed. The carpet in the hall was deep burgundy and very thick. 'You carry on with the skirting boards.' Hope just nodded, avoiding eye contact as she knelt down with her duster. Lisa polished a mahogany side table and came to a full-length bronze mirror which stood next to a doorway. This was the room that 'Lady Muck' hadn't wanted cleaned. Lisa wondered what was on the other side of the door. The loud clattering noise from inside the room made her jump. She hesitated, listening for another noise. There was silence. She reached out her hand slowly towards the antique metal door handle. The slender fingers that gently touched her shoulder made her drop her polish in shock. Estelle Rycroft was standing right behind her, smiling.

'The library looks much better. I was wondering if you and Hope could make a start in the drawing room. I have friends coming over tonight.'

Lisa nodded, 'I thought I heard something in the room ...'

'That room's empty. It's just a guest room.' Estelle's smile faded slightly. 'If you could start on the drawing room . . .'

The question hung in the air, sounding more like a demand with each passing second.

The drawing room was more lavishly furnished than the other rooms. There was a huge open fire burning on one wall, acting as a centrepiece to the room. It was sculpted from black marble, with snakes carved up each side. Then she saw the plant to the left of the fireplace. It looked like a vine, with thick white runners trailing up the wall. There were flowers that looked like lilies growing along each vine and small, dark-red berries that hung in tight clusters. She stood there for a second, taking it in. The thicker stems lower down had red veins that stood out from the milk-white stalks. The flowers were mostly white in colour, but had pink and red mixed into the edges of the petals. The container that the plant was in was perhaps even more interesting. It was about three-feet long and about eighteen inches wide and looked to be made from some sort of metal. The box was crudely made, but was *very* old. In colour it was a cross between silver and pewter. With the soil it had inside, it would probably take two men to lift it. She tried to guess what it was. Perhaps some kind of medieval treasure chest?

The outside of the box was engraved with some sort of complex design. Lisa took a step closer. It had a swirling pattern that stood out from the side of the box. She couldn't quite make it out. The more she looked at it, the less clear it became. In addition to this, there was a smell to the plant that Lisa recognised. It was an unpleasant odour that reminded her of rotten meat. The idea of spraying the plant with air freshener ran through her mind when she suddenly remembered the stained glass window in the library. This was the plant in the window! The pattern caught her eye again, the swirls seeming to come together to form shapes …

'I thought you might be thirsty. I made you some drinks.' Estelle drifted into the room and Hope jumped up so quickly her earphones fell out. Estelle placed a tray of drinks on the table and gestured for the cleaners to sit on the sofa.

'I was looking at your plant, I've not seen one of those before.' Lisa took a sip of her coffee.

Estelle smiled more broadly, 'Yes, I had it imported. It's very old. Not as old as the box though.' Estelle's bright hazel eyes seemed to scan Lisa's face, looking for some sign of emotion.

'Where's it from?'

'Oh … it's just something I picked up from my travels. I collect old items. You could call it my hobby.' Estelle lifted a crystal glass filled with red liquid. 'You can distil a liquor from the berries of that plant.' She raised the glass by way of example. 'It's quite delicious.'

A rustling noise made the cleaners look up. Lisa saw movement on one of the vine's white branches. A tiny white and red bird hopped along the vine. It was quickly joined by two others that emerged from behind one of the flowers.

'Ahhh … my babies!' Estelle's face lit up with delight as she extended her slim right arm. One of the birds jumped from the vine, fluttering down towards her. It stopped in front of her hand, hovering like a hummingbird. Lisa could hear the frantic beat of its tiny wings and was amazed, but began to feel queasy. 'These are my other hobby, my finches. I breed them myself in my aviary. I think they're hungry. Are you hungry my babies?'

Estelle talked to them like children and two more hopped off the plant and took to flight. Lisa saw more of them jostling for space near the ceiling. She noticed the peculiar shape of the one hovering by Estelle's hand. It had a body like a bird, but its beak was long and very sharp. In fact, its face didn't look like a bird at all. It reminded her of a prawn. It had scrawny legs, like some small lizard, dangling beneath its body.

Estelle turned towards Hope. 'Could you be a dear and feed my finches? They look hungry.'

Hope silently stood and rolled up the sleeves of her shirt as high as they would go. Lisa looked frantically around the room, her eyes once again alighting on the box. The design was human figures, screaming faces and torn limbs. She could make out horned devils and torsos skewered with pitchforks and lances. It was a vision of Hell.

The bird near Estelle flew over to Hope, landing on her right forearm. Two more birds landed on her other arm, whilst another hovered by her neck. The first stuck its beak into her skin like a needle. As if this were a signal the birds all drove their beaks into the girl's flesh as more of them fluttered down to feed.

Lisa struggled to her feet and felt like she was going to vomit. She stumbled into the table and staggered towards the arch. She ran wildly down the hallway, crashing into a full-length mirror, groping blindly for the front door. She found a door handle and ran through it, her head swimming. She hit something, knocking it over. The sight before her made her scream.

She was standing in the forbidden downstairs bedroom. Lying on the bed, strapped firmly down, was Margie Smith. Every inch of her exposed body covered with puncture marks. Between the matted locks of grey hair that masked her face, Lisa could see that the woman's eyes had been pecked out. Her stomach gave up its fight and her legs gave way beneath her.

'Lisa.' The voice softly coaxed her from unconsciousness. 'Lisa.' Her eyes slowly opened. Estelle sat opposite her with Hope by her side, two birds still feeding on her arm. The young girl was covered in puncture wounds. 'Are you familiar with the legend of Pandora's box, Lisa?' Estelle took a sip from her glass. Lisa felt herself drifting into shock. One of the birds flew from Hope's arm and hovered in front of the plant, moving closer to the flower. It probed its long beak into the bloom, injecting some of the blood into the centre of the petals. The red veins spread further down the stem with this new infusion.

'Pandora had a box Lisa … a box she should never have opened. Inside were creatures that swept the ancient world like a plague.' Estelle nodded towards the metal box then leaned forward. 'But my name wasn't really Pandora. Like with Chinese whispers, these stories change over time. But I struck a bargain with them. Immortality if I keep both them and the tree of life well fed. Look at it as the best gardening job in history.' Her laughter seemed to echo in Lisa's head. 'Young Hope here is my watering can … my little helper.' She stroked Hope's hand lovingly. The girl seemed to be engrossed in feeding the creatures from her wrist.

Estelle smiled one last time and made a clucking sound. Lisa heard the frantic beating of wings, then felt tiny clawed feet moving over her body. The last thing she saw were the eager, tiny, black eyes swarming around her face.

THE GHOST IN THE GRANDFATHER CLOCK
Robert D Hayward

'Dad, do tell us the story of Cottlesdon Manor!' begged young Simon. 'Who's haunting this old house, and why?'

'Simon, I don't think this is quite the time to -'

'No, we must face this thing squarely,' broke in John Findlay, interrupting his wife Biddy's nervous twittering. 'It's all nonsense, of course; but it's best to be prepared. Briefly then, this manor was once owned by a rich baronet called Sir Horatio Plonk.' He frowned at his son, who grinned at the name, and then he went on. 'Just over a hundred years ago, Sir Horatio was murdered by his own butler - for his money, apparently - and his body was hidden in the old grandfather clock. This is said to have happened one Sunday night, and the story goes that every Sunday night, at midnight, his ghost comes out of the clock to terrorise the house's inhabitants until the early hours of Monday morning.'

'Was the body ever found?' Biddy chirruped anxiously. 'Because if it was - oh dear! *that* may confirm the ghost story.'

'Oh, they found the body, all right - on the floor of the grandfather clock. And they found the rope he had been strangled with, all but a frayed end that had apparently been cut off to make a stronger knot. But they never found the butler; he just vanished abroad somewhere with the money. And that's all there is to it.'

'Sunday night. That's tomorrow night,' twittered Biddy. 'Oh, children, do be careful.'

'So he's coming out tomorrow night!' said Simon boldly. 'Well, all I can say is: I'll be waiting for him with a pillow.'

'Me too!' chimed in his younger sister Debbie. 'I want to find out whether it will go through him.'

John Findlay remembered these words when he was lying awake with Biddy the following night - their first Sunday night in Cottlesdon Manor. They had both agreed to keep vigil so that they could protect their children if necessary.

Midnight was approaching, and Cottlesdon Manor was shrouded in a cloak of intense brooding gloom. The very air seemed to tingle, and an eerie sensation began to creep up John's spine; it was as though some great drama was about to be enacted below.

The witching hour arrived, and the sound of the old grandfather clock in the hall downstairs echoed strangely round the ancient manor house as its mournful gong-like boom slowly began to strike midnight. But tonight the chimes had a peculiar vibrating quality to them, and the moment they had died out John and Biddy thought they heard a low, but sinister creaking sound - rather like the sound of an old wooden door swinging open on its hinges. Seconds later they heard loud whispering from outside, from a little way along the corridor; and there were surreptitious footsteps on the stairs. John got out of bed immediately and Biddy, more cautiously, arose and followed him to the bedroom door.

'I didn't like the sound of those chimes at all!' Biddy chirruped in mounting nervous tension as they stole out into the corridor leading to the great winding stairway. 'And what was that strange creaking?'

'I don't know,' replied John softly, 'but if there's any danger to the children we must get them - and ourselves - out as soon as possible. I was talking to the local vicar the other day, and he's quite willing to take us in for the night.'

John and Biddy reached the head of the stairs and, looking down the ancient winding staircase, saw a pair of red-robed figures on the stairs, one holding a pillow. Almost at the same moment the hall below was illuminated by a vivid, whitish blue light, like that produced by lightning, and a hollow groan echoed through the old manor house. The figures on the stairs both screamed and then came pelting back up the stairs as fast as their legs could carry them. Slow labouring footsteps could now be heard climbing towards them, accompanied by heavy breathing; and all four of them ran for their lives, tripping over the landing carpet as they dashed through the corridor and past the bedrooms.

'Quick, children; down the back stairs!' cried John Findlay, while Biddy hurriedly shepherded Simon and Debbie to the far end of the corridor, where a dark passage led to a flight of wooden steps. They all clattered down these and let themselves out by one of the back doors.

They ran across moonlit fields and meadows towards the vicarage, which nestled beside the village church. The vicar was still up when they arrived and he let them in straight away.

'I thought you'd come tonight,' he welcomed them, half anxious, half relieved, as he showed them into his main sitting room, 'this being the night of the ghost.'

'What on earth's going on?' John gasped as soon as they had crowded in and sat down. 'I didn't believe in all that nonsense about ghosts, but now ...'

'Oh, that manor house is haunted, all right!' said the vicar with a shudder. 'You're only one of several dozen families who have come and gone from that accursed place, and I know I wouldn't -'

'Well, we haven't gone yet!' John broke in determinedly. 'But we can't go on like this, having to spend the night out every Sunday. What do you suggest we do?'

The vicar thought for a moment. 'The only thing I can think of is to try and exorcise the ghost,' he said at last. 'As it happens, the new rector of the neighbouring parish has some experience in exorcism; and I know him quite well. Shall I call him up for you?'

'First thing in the morning.' In his eagerness John fell over his words. 'Meanwhile, we're really grateful to you for your hospitality.'

'I can only offer you the garret room and one small bedroom,' said the vicar, 'but they're quite comfortable.'

John and Biddy chose the bedroom, partly because the children both clamoured for the garret; and they were soon all in bed and fast asleep.

In the morning the vicar contacted the young rector he had spoken of, and everything was soon arranged. The rector would spend the following Sunday evening with them, and then they would all wait up for the ghost and confront him if he showed up again at midnight.

It was with many strange and terrifying thoughts that the family gathered in Cottlesdon Manor's ornate sitting room on that second Sunday night, leaving the door wide open so that the outline of the old grandfather clock out in the hall was framed in the doorway. The vicar and the rector sat in armchairs on either side of the settee, John and Biddy sat on the settee itself and the children hid behind it, peeping out excitely over its plush upholstery.

Midnight approached, and the ancient manor house was enveloped in a black velvet pall, except for one thin shaft of moonlight that fell slantwise across the old grandfather clock. Everyone waited with bated breath, and as the clock began to whirr in readiness for striking midnight, a chill ran up and down their spines and their hair seemed to stand on end.

A series of slow gong-like booms reverberated through the house as the ancient timepiece chimed midnight. The first four chimes, eerie enough, sounded quite ordinary; but then they took on a strange unearthly tone, vibratory and hollow, growing distinctly louder as they reached nine and ten. No sooner had the last stroke of midnight sounded than there came a soft click, followed by a creaking noise; and the door of the old grandfather clock swung open on its hinges before their very eyes. The interior of the clock glowed a vivid electric blue, which lit up the entire hall and sitting room, and within this lurid light the outlines of a ghostly figure began to form.

Within seconds the contours had hardened into the terrifying spectre of an old man, tall but hideously bent over on one side, with close-cropped hair and ghastly staring eyes aglow with red light. He was robed from head to foot in a thick whitish blue gown with deep folds, through which the onlookers could still see the intricate woodwork of the grandfather clock. He was transparent, and yet not transparent; 'translucent' would have been a better word for it. But what was the children's terror when the apparition stepped right out of the grandfather clock and moved slowly towards them, spectral hands outstretched!

Biddy shrank back in fright, and both children cowered out of sight behind the settee. John Findlay, gazing in fascinated horror at the phantom, was riveted by the expression of intense anguish in its glaring eyes; and the vicar particularly noticed that around its neck ran a hideous black mark - the mark of a rope.

'The gallows!' he whispered in a hoarse croak as the spectre glided inexorably towards them. An unspeakable dread now seized them all. The phantom floated over the carpet without seeming to touch it; and yet they heard, quite unmistakably, the sound of its footsteps - hollow and echoing, as though it were walking on bare wood. They all recoiled in terror; and as Sir Horatio Plonk's ghost bore down on them, its breathing grew heavy and jerky, and its eyes were suddenly filled with an expression of the utmost evil.

The apparition was almost upon them when the rector, sensing even in his horror that their very souls were in danger, leapt to his feet and held aloft a small wooden cross which he had brought with him.

'Be gone, evil spirit!' he cried out in a loud febrile voice, using the cross to ward off the phantom as its outstretched hands reached out to clamp themselves round his neck. 'In the name of Jesus Christ, I command you to leave Cottlesdon Manor and enter it no more.'

Three things happened simultaneously. A long blood-curdling shriek rent the air, heart-rending yet inhuman; the ghost dissolved into thin air; and a tremendous cracking sound came from the hall. Silence then descended as the house, relieved of its horrors, was plunged into darkness; and its ancient rooms revived as if a breath of fresh air had rushed into them from outside. It was only now that they noticed that the old grandfather clock had stopped ticking.

The first thing John Findlay did was switch on the lights. Biddy had fainted, but when she was brought round they all thanked the rector for their deliverance. None of them were in any doubt that the ghost had been exorcised, and that Cottlesdon Manor was now really theirs.

'Dad, look at the old grandfather clock!' cried out young Simon.

Everyone looked, and saw that the clock's ornate wooden casing was split down the middle. The door still swung open, but the ancient timepiece was now grotesquely bent over into a peculiar likeness of the old man's ghost. The dial was cracked and several of its great Roman numerals hung loose. And now, as they approached, John pointed to something that lay on the floor of the casing, right at the back - an object half hidden in the deepest corner of the old grandfather clock.

He reached in, retrieved it and held it up for them all to see.

It was a short coil of rope, frayed at one end; and it was tied into a noose.

A GHOST'S STORY
Peter Schapira (12)

Where out of the darkness white meets white,
When expelled from the mind is out of sight,
When soundless to listening ears,
The mind is too numb to fight.
Dark dreams haunt the deepest recesses of the mind and
We sometimes see what we do not want to find.

When they cut me I did not feel anything. Ghosts do not feel. Souls only sense a happening. Something shimmers through you, whispers past you and then overcomes you. There is nothing tangible. You are a breath of air. In the light we cannot see each other, but in the silent dark you are never alone. You can see your hands, but you cannot touch. You can see your feet, but you do not feel the ground beneath them. The air may be cold and damp, but you do not shiver. It is the heat of a summer's day that you have to be afraid of.

You only eat and sleep in the minds of others. As I have grown older I go for days and days without eating, only waking fitfully, snatching a few seconds of existence in the twilight hours.

My brother and I were joined. With one heart we shared everything. For six months we lived as one. We wore the same clothes. We laughed and cried together. We played and fed together. If one of us was ill, so was the other one. If one was upset, the other felt it. We were two parts of the same whole. But we did not grow up together. He was always bigger and stronger. To gain a son they would lose a son. Death was preferable to life. For them the decision seemed easy and with it I was born in an instant.

There is a dull fizzing. An ache that has never left me: why did they choose him over me? What right did they have to choose between us? They could not be sure that in casting one half away the other would stay. But all too soon the ashen-drawn faces, tear-stained and lined, eased and changed. Watching them in the clinical light of day, as they sat with my brother in the hospital, I saw how they poured their future into him. I became the past. They took comfort in his new found strength. He soon began to crawl and then to walk and talk.

In those days I was never far away. My mother would be sitting in the garden on a soft, brightly coloured rug and my brother would be crawling in the grass. Rolling a yellow ball towards him, she would stop suddenly and looking somewhere towards me, eyes flitting, focusing on a nothingness, she would call out, 'Are you there? What are you doing? Go away!' An ice-cold shrill shriek splitting the air. Such cruelty. And then she would scoop up my brother and rush indoors, leaving me again.

Now that I had her, I would not leave my mother alone. Washing up after dinner she would see me in the half-light and drop a glass or plate. 'Cursed thing!' she would cry bitterly, and then find solace in my father's arms or in my brother's shining baby face. And then in the very heart of the night when darkness blankets everything I would be there. She hid her bedside photos of me in the hope that I would not come. But I would slip in and out of the sheets with ease, my face pressed up close against hers. Then I could sense her anguish and her guilt. She would turn into her pillow and try to block me out, but I would keep on coming back until, swollen eyelids closed, she fell asleep.

I am happy at the pain I caused.

They never told my brother that he shared his birth. For thirteen years they have kept it a secret. Tomorrow he will no longer be a child.

Something stirred. In the pitch-dark he heard a sound. Creeping back under the blankets he curled up into a small ball. Feline. He thought the sound went away. But then he felt something trickle down his spine. A cold, clammy, spindly finger, playing with the wisps on the back of his neck. Rats in the pillow tugging at his short curly hair.

A creak from under the bed. He shut his eyes. But they stayed open. In the darkness he was sure he saw something move. Shadows danced outside. They seemed to stretch out their hands and open the window. Falling, he felt himself letting out a silent shout. Twisting the bedclothes around himself, he found that he was writhing in a pit of slithering snakes. Hissing, spitting at his every move he could not escape the slitted whites of their eyes. His chest tightened and a searing pain shot through his body. He could not breathe. Gasping, he twisted and turned in the muddy darkness. Shadows moved beneath him. Coughing and spluttering he felt himself hauled back upwards. He lay on his side rasping for air … and then he felt the ice-cold air tickle his feet.

I sat at the end of my brother's bed and watched him. In the silence, tranquillity returned and he gently rolled over in his sleep, the pretty face glistening as the moonlight broke through the shuttered window. I saw my hand brush his cheek and play with his hair. I lay down next to him. He shivered. I wanted to play with him again but I could not feel a thing. I could not even cry. At that moment he opened his eyes and looked straight at me.

'Who are you?' he asked in a matter of fact way, and then quickly losing his confidence whispered, 'you look like me.'

'Your brother,' I heard myself say. It was the first time I had ever spoken and I sounded like him. 'They never told you.'

He did not seem surprised, but rather moved himself towards me. I did not know what to do. I just lay there next to him and let him clasp the air beside him.

'I think I always knew that there was something,' he said suddenly, sitting up and pointing at the long scar down the centre of his chest. 'At times I have felt that there were two of me, but friends just laughed and said I was being stupid. It was like there was a shadow to myself but I have never seen you before. What is it like to be dead?'

'Being dead'. as he had so crudely put it, was not something I had ever really thought about.

'Asleep, not existing, wasted. But how can I be 'dead' if you are talking to me, if you can see me?'

My brother opened his mouth to ask another question and then shut it again. And then the floodgates opened, question after question in quick succession tumbled out. Where did I live? What did I do all day? Had anybody else seen me? Was it cold? Was it lonely? What did I eat? Did I have friends and go out to play? ... My answers, slow and simple, puzzled him. I lived where he lived and slept unless he was awake when sleeping. He flopped back down on his pillow staring straight up at the ceiling.

After some time he asked abruptly, 'Why did you come now? It's my birthday tomorrow.'

'Our birthday,' I retorted sharply.

'I never thought ghosts had birthdays.'

'Why not? I have two: the one I share with you when we were born sewn together and the other when we were ripped apart. The only difference is that you can celebrate yours and I can't.'

'Well, why did you come tonight? I really want tomorrow.'

'You want to grow up that quickly? I came so that you would understand the truth. I mean no harm to you. I exist in the deepest recesses of your mind, where, at certain times in your life, you will step inside and find me waiting for you. You must live your life.'

'And you contend with your death.' My twin brother had completed my sentence.

In the morning they found him lying as we had always lain when we were together: a mirrored indentation of his self in the sheets by his side. I was watching.

OTHERWORLDLY

(A short fantasy built around an old house which once stood in Windsor Street, Dundee)

Mhairi Jarvis

Imposingly large and impressively desolate was the old house's demeanour as I recall seeing it through ten-year-old eyes, even when swathed in sunshine. With its broad shoulders draped in red and green mottled, bare space dotted ivy, it was reminiscent of a well born, mature lady wearing her patchily moth-eaten fur shoulder cape with pride.

It had a sinister reputation acquired via its contrasting, even creepier image which it was capable of conjuring during winter's long-lasting dark hours, when it would loom in the darkness, lending alarm to all forced to cross its sparsely lit path. Many people, through many years had complained of suffering uncanny experiences within its vicinity, although no actual recorded proof of such ever existed.

I, myself, though, am forced to admit to a belief that the area in which it stood was, and, perhaps still is, a time zone where I slipped from one time, one world to another at least twice. I came to no harm, but was brought to the opinion that it is man - the despoiler - who is mostly to be feared.

There was what one might describe as an element of weirdness in my attraction to the house, an odd kind of love such as one feels for a favourite, elderly relative and, I suppose, I believed it to reciprocate the feeling.

Steadfastly immovable, it jealously guarded a dozen or so allotments over which it towered, presumably a metamorphosis of its own, once fine, velvet green lawns, while it observed the antics of children, like myself, who gathered in its area, luxuriating in the freedom allocated during the too short, summer holidays from school.

I myself imagined the house to have been built, originally, as a large, farmhouse-type dwelling for a wealthy landowner, with twenty or thirty much smaller, humble abodes, for those who could afford them, on the opposite side of the street. They had, of course, by my childhood, benefited by extensive renovation.

The passing of time, approach of industry and encroachment of town upon country may have seen the house, later, providing a home for a well-off mill owner, with the smaller houses let at exorbitant rents to those of his workers who could, only just, afford to inhabit them as there were, at one time, several mills in the town, all of which ended up as derelict as the poor house.

Whichever, I felt sad for the house and had a fantasy that one day I would be rich enough to buy it. I would never have been afraid to live in the house - never be deterred by the stories.

Surrounded by three counties and a river, the house enjoyed views of forestry, hills and fields containing various types and colours of livestock, visible only as specks on the landscape. A ferry trip across the silvery river or a rail trip across the bridge which spanned it was a much looked forward to treat to us children, bringing us closer to the prospect the house would continually enjoy. From our side of the river the view was that of a black, white and brown-speckled, lumpy, bumpy patchwork quilt. Country life on the edge of town.

Despite the tales of the house's disposition, we children played our games within its vicinity, fearlessly, blissfully unaware of invisible entities, within its walls, interned from the sun watching us. I believe that the stories were invented to compensate for the dearth of knowledge of the house's authentic history, spread by people over the years to fertilise the tales, as farmers spread fruitful substances over their land in the hope of better crops.

The street in which the house stood was a long, wide avenue, not so much tree lined as, indiscriminately, tree dotted. It stretched, with a little tug, from a very busy road which was once a toll road in the days of horse and carriage travel, down to the silvery river.

Along with the love I felt for the house, there also existed within me a gnawing hunger to know it better, and, although rarely do any of us obtain fulfilment of our dreams, I am convinced that I did. If inanimate objects have the soul to communicate, then I know that the house read my thoughts and granted me a long drawn-out few seconds into its private lives, its other days, and gave me the gift of seeing some of my own.

It was an extremely hot, static summer's day, and, feeling too drained and exhausted for games, I stood rooted, mesmerised by the house's mysticism and the sun's hazy shine. The house was shimmering, as if submerged in water, and, to my amazement, I saw my surroundings alter, and, become otherworldly.

I saw small boys in breeches to the knee, and little girls in ground-swishing dresses playing together, arguing politely, aggression free, as they frolicked on velvet smooth lawns. Enthralled, I watched what I assumed were milkmaids toiling beneath the hot sun, toting huge wooden pails of frothy milk. The house beamed with happiness and quivered with activity as people hurried about their tasks, as busy as the multitudinous bees which flitted from flower to flower in a golden glow of a honey dripping atmosphere.

I had been shifted in time to stand amidst an assortment of quaint scenes and visions wherein pale-skinned ladies, sheltering beneath parasols, leant on the arms of elegantly attired gentlemen as they strolled across the lawns, passed by the romping children and some enticing, happy, healthy, small spaniel-type dogs, and made their way through black, wrought iron gates into the street. I sensed affluence as I watched black and brown horses with pelts like mirrors draw carriages over a hard-packed mud driveway into the same streets. They were so close, I could have touched them.

Outside the gates people ambled and chatted while children played various games. One boy came running down the street chasing an iron hoop, hitting it with a poker-type implement. Suddenly it fell and clattered against some railings, startling me, and, all the movement evolved into slow motion, as if time were becoming a luxury. Everything was fading, but not before, just for an instance, one of the small girls stood up and turned to look in my direction. Except for the clothes, she was me!

My eyes were waterlogged, so that I had to blink, and, when I looked again, I focused on the poor old derelict. I shivered, suddenly cold, and noticed that the sun had gone behind a cloud. Although disappointed I was comforted to know that the house had once been loved and useful. Had it been fancy or had I been privileged?

The second vision, four decades later, left me feeling much more uneasy. It was, once again, a very hot summer's day, and, being in the locality, I decided to indulge my nostalgic bent and visit my dear old, much maligned friend, perhaps with the help of the sun, lend it a few precious, long drawn-out seconds of life again, but, to my chagrin and heart-wrenching disappointment, it was gone, had become, I presumed, a victim of official vandalism.

In its place stood row upon row of small houses, characterless little boxes in comparison to my majestic friend. A lump rose in my throat, and I sighed inwardly - 'My dear old friend, I let you down. Where was

I all these years when you needed me? I was in that other land, that other world of growing up and forgetting. I neglected you! I should have been here for you, should have stopped them! Dear old house, if you are still aware, in another time, please know, that, whenever I have a mind to, I can rebuild you in my mind's eye, in my heart, in my soul. Goodbye old friend' ... and, turning ruefully to leave, I caught sight of a young girl, about ten-years-old, strangely attired, a futuristic child, transfixed, mesmerised by the sun's shimmering haze, appearing to be seeing unfamiliar things happening, perhaps before her time, in small houses the like of which she had not seen, built decades before her birth.

Then, before my eyes the houses began to crumble to dust and to be slowly replaced by tall, thick concrete towers, dense and windowless. There was nothing else to be seen, no river, no grass, nothing green at all, only the depressing grey towers. Just for an instant I thought I saw something, a slimy, slithering, horrible creeping thing. I turned to look behind me and saw nothing but greyness, an impenetrable, smoggy greyness. I felt, rather than saw two figures looming through it. As they came closer, and I could distinguish more, I noticed that they were wearing thin, see-through masks over their mouths and noses. I turned slowly full circle. There was nothing to be seen, no patchwork quilt, no sun, no clear atmosphere to be felt. There was only that airless indescribable nothing!

I could not draw breath! Maybe the masks they wore provided air! I closed my eyes and prayed for aid, and, when I opened them again, to my intense relief, the sun shone brightly, and the air was crystal clear, sweet and clean. I relished a deep, deep breath.

Then, I saw the girl, still there, startled by, no doubt, and full of wonder at the vision, afraid and yet, being succumbed by the succulent horror. She must have been so frightened at the sight of the grass, the river, the patchwork quilt. Perhaps the word green was not even in her day's vocabulary. Her wonderment would have been greater than mine, if she had never known the likes of the small houses. I wondered about her world, until, with sudden realisation, fear seized my soul, for fleetingly, I had glimpsed it. Unexpectedly, she turned to look in my direction and my heart all but stopped. I should have known, should have expected it - even with the mask on, I recognised, me!

Once again sheer panic gripped my soul when I remembered the slimy, slithering thing.

The river! The beautiful, silvery river!

Was that what the house had tried to do all through its years of distrust? Had people really been privileged? Was the house revealing past, present and future to all of us, but being human we were - frightened ... so, had to destroy?

Epilogue

Now, as I stand at my window enjoying a view that would melt the hardest heart, I remember how, more than forty years ago, the view would not have been quite as clear as my childhood may have imagined, for the air had been polluted by smoke from all the mill chimneys. We had just grown so accustomed to it, we saw through it!

That atmosphere had been cleared. That world had been saved.

Is Man still capable of learning, or have we become just too complacent? Would all the world's 'times' be saved, or are we, the despoilers, on our last chance?

I'm old now and less inclined to travel to the house's vicinity to find out!

I look at the patchwork quilt and the river. There are some small towns on the landscape now, but the quilt is shrinking. Soon, it may not exist if that future is coming, is encroaching. If that horrendous, mask wearing future is ... coming!

Dirt Clad Window
Michael Hurst

It's a long way back, without a road map or directions. Longing for the comfort of home for such a long time now, although I do not know for how long as the days passed without knowledge or care?

The area around proved a secure environment as the small wooden house stood in the clearing within a secluded wood with plenty of opportunities for food and water nearby. Looking through the window of the house brought lush green fields on the outskirts of the wood and gracefully climbing mountains peaked with white snow to the eyes. The repairs took some time since I stumbled across this place and such things as plumbing seemed non-existent. After this there were still many other problems that came from the woodwork, so to say, after spending time here; the problems being some large and small holes protruding through the wooden beams, which make up the roof and the entirety of the house which I have claimed as my own.

Three months in and I have kept myself busy. Every day there has been something that needed my full attention, normally delaying a list of backlogged problems that neither bothered me nor stressed me. Since there has been no distractions the amount of work that has been invested into the house has been immense and now it is complete.

The days seem empty. I have nothing to do. I rarely venture out, unless for food or water. I lie here, in this bed, I'm starring through the dirt clad window. Actually, I cannot remember the comforts of home, only hazed recollections rise in my thoughts and in pictures of the night. What I long for is change or even company, if only to get rid of the vermin, which sits upon my empty bookcase.

To think of this isolation turns the front of my heart to lead, it leaning forward, pressing against the rib cage. With each breath the weight increases, collecting a life of feeling and memory and compressing it into a black hole. A creak can be heard as it pushes and breaks free from its shell. As I long to do. I will it to be free, to leave this body of mine. I breathe faster and heavier than before till I am blind from pain. Each millimetre rips the flesh around this now lead ball, tearing its way through till it breaks free of its cage. Pushing the skin out without ripping it, the bones of the chest extend beyond their boundaries. Looking down at this misshapen mess I decide that this is the moment, the time to set my heart free. Kneeling on my bed I lean further forward, placing my head upon the mattress and gripping the wooden post. With one last deep breathe, I scream.

Every muscle in this frail body begins to contract with immense tension. Breaking more bones it moves slightly forward and finally begins to tear the skin. A small stream of blood pours onto the bed and drips rhythmically upon the floor, replacing the beat of my weak heart. 'Once more,' I say to myself, 'just one more.'

One quick, sharp inhalation brought pain of which I have never experienced in this life. Within one second my life ended. The little support the broken bones gave, now gave way; tearing the skin and releasing a flood of blood onto the bed. I could not let go of the wooden post. Then a feeling of relief rushed through me, losing the weight from inside my chest; the iron ball could not be seen as it left my body through the torrent of blood. It was over. There was a crash as the ball broke through the bed and a screeching sound of it travelling to the floor, eventually breaking through the floor. I was jerked down, my body smashing against the mattress. The weight so immense pulled at every tendon in this shell and I used what little strength I had left and pushed myself away from the bed, hoping to snap the ties which bound me to this ball; only to feel a movement from inside, deep inside.

Feeling numb and coughing up what remained of my blood, I felt my innards rush through the hole left by my heart; shredding what was left of my skin, snapping my sternum and releasing the gates to my body. Indescribable, flesh of the likes that I have never witnessed, nor will I ever witness passed before my sight. Feeling my intestine slowly moving upwards from within the confines of my mortal coil. Like pulling wet string through the tight grip of your hand. A queer feeling of vomiting air came from within. One last jerk hit my body as the last of my entrails pulled me to the bed, the weight of the ball increasing, screaming; I closed my eyes, darkness, pain as it slowly tore from me, then snap. I was free.

A raven perched upon the corner of the bookcase and looked longingly at my body and the scene that had unfolded. Thick, dark red blood crept along the wooden floorboards, taking a few moments to pass over each board. The only noise that could be heard was the faint tapping of the blood splashing from the bed to the floor.

Outstretched, open eyed and with what seemed like a faint smile, the raven flew over to me and perched upon the wooden bedposts. It sat there for some time as if in deep contemplation, bobbing its head up and down and then staring, the raven gracefully floated down to the floor. With every hop the raven waited for a brief moment looking in all directions, tilting its head to the right, and began to hop closer still to the flesh lying on the floor. It began picking pieces up, looking bemused at what it played with but completely enthralled. Then it looked towards me, interested in the reflection of itself in my clouded eyes it jumped up and sat, staring, looking at a companion in white. It leaned in and jabbed furiously at the reflection it had seen.

Nothing could stop the sheer aggression pulsating through its primitive mind. Such single mindedness can be dangerous. It stopped only to clean the clear solution that smothered its beak, eyes and trickled down off its body. Then the raven began to struggle and cough, black plumes thrown from its body. Screeching as its eyes began to bulge from its cranium, one last stab of its black beak pierced through the soft tissue of my eye taking it from the socket as pulled back. Then it fell limp in the grip of my hand. I felt a strange feeling, contracting of the muscles in my face. I ... I ... I think? Yes, I am smiling.

GRIN
Barry Woods

I stayed on familiar roads, kept checking my pocket to ensure the coins were safe. Nobody knew of them, not even my brother Theo; he'd have slit my throat and left me for the dogs like the others - they were more needy street-beggars you see, or so they kept whining. I tried to ignore their leering from dark corners. Behind me the crash of horses' hooves slammed on cobblestones. I looked around and saw a coach driver whipping fierily at the reigns.

'Out of the way, gutter rat!' he yelled.

The wobbly carriage passed by, its wheels splashing me with grime. I jumped out of the way like a scared dog and noticed the lord and lady aboard wore the fancy clothes and tall hats. Inside they turned their heads away, not wishing to spare me a glance.

Gazing up over smoky rooftops, I caught the sun's glow before it dropped into dusk.

When I reached Pillars Lane it was dark. A green sign for the Dog and Whistle rocked gently on its hinges. I could hear a piano tinkling inside. I thought a stiff whisky would have eased my anxiety but no, not a penny could be squandered. I dawdled past the doors catching a whiff of the ale smells. A fat dog was slumped on the step; he didn't even lift his head. I pulled out the address from my pocket and looked at the creased paper and the numbers 76A, that street behind the inn; that back-street many of us had known about. I could see a yellow light burning up there in the top window.

The steps up to the doorway were steep. The red door looked newly painted. I pulled at the bell handle, sent it tinkling and swinging and the door creaked open. He stood there with his hair tied back in a small tail.

'You … again,' he said.

I pushed the coins into his hand. He counted them out carefully, all professional like, same as the lords and ladies.

'I'm impressed; took you long enough, though.'

He welcomed me inside and I followed him up two flights of stairs. At the top he paused and glanced back at me; he reached into the pockets of his waistcoat and pulled out a brass key. The door struggled to open but soon did and I was in the attic, the room with the burning light all cold and eerie. He strode over and released the catch on the open window letting the heavy pane drop with a thump. The curtains settled.

'The chair, please,' he said.

I sat down in a high backed chair and watched as he tied a stained apron across his groin. He put gloves on and reached for a leather strap, which fastened over the back of the chair and across my chest.

'... So you don't ruin the procedure.'

I nodded.

He turned his back and started taking things out from a cabinet. He threw the lid off a bottle, took a gulp then looked back to me.

'Let's make this quick,' he said wiping his mouth. It was alcohol. I could smell it.

He placed a tray of utensils on a sideboard then, pressing one hand on my forehead, pushed my head back into the pallid light of the lamp. I stared at the ceiling for a second ... then it began. Cold steel incised my top lip and surrounding tissue. I screamed and kicked my legs in agony. The jerky movements made my eyes water as the sharp knife serrated flesh all the way around my mouth. I felt the cold, cruel instrument slice violently through the thicker flesh of my cheek ripping and widening my mouth up to the earlobe, dragging my head sideways. Again, he slashed the other cheek with such force it felt loose and exposed, and the blood dripped from my chin like a slow running tap. He threw alcohol onto the wound - a sharper sting. Wiping his forehead he took another swig from the bottle. I saw the fresh blood splats on his apron. He swapped the knife for a different tool and jammed the next pick-like object up into my gums and started to hack and tear at the flesh between my teeth. It ground on the enamel beneath.

'Keep your head still! This is just as hard for me.'

I closed my damp eyes in horror and waited for it to end, but the gum tissue didn't fall away easily. He poured another measure of alcohol onto me; I squealed and panted and shook my head with nervous rage.

The special surgeon stood back for a second and admired his work. Then he held a mirror to me ... I looked in to the grim reflection and gasped: no matter which expression I forced, death's toothy grin spread from ear to ear; I was a vision of the living dead, of the ultimate freak.

He bandaged me up and pulled my spent body from the chair.

'Let it settle for a week,' he said. 'When folk cast their eyes on you now … well, they'll gladly pay you to get out of their sights - you shall never go hungry again.'

ESCAPE
Tracey Douglas

Friday 10 December

Dear Friend,

I am writing this to you in a hurried fashion because I know I have not long left on this plain. I will not exist in the morning. Already the sun has closed its eyes and the dark rim of shade is beginning to sadden the sky. I meet my doom knowingly and unafraid. I do not have the strength or will to fight any more. I hope after hearing my tale you will forgive me for my sweet surrender ...

I arose Wednesday morning after a disturbed night's sleep feeling lethargic and sick. The lingering memories of a dream unnerved me. I dreamt someone or thing had been in my room. I had not seen them but in a trance-like state had smelt and sensed an unnatural presence. The sickly sweet intoxicating smell remained in my nostrils all day preventing me from eating. By bedtime I was exhausted and fell immediately into a deep slumber. Whilst in this drowsy state I imagined a green mist penetrating my window and creeping slowly towards my bed. The sweet exhilarating smell grew stronger. I was paralysed but oddly unafraid. I tried in vain to open my eyes. I felt a face staring at me, its cold black eyes boring into my head. The blank dead eyes seemed to be trying to penetrate my thoughts. The face seemed strangely familiar. I imagined icy fingers turning my head to expose my neck. I felt a dull pain then images of monstrous abominations flashed through my mind. Collected memories of an ancient race unfolded in my consciousness and untold tales of horror began to be exposed to me. My meaningless tales of life were nothing compared to these wretched horrors. I wanted to scream but no sound came out.

After these horrors a calm sea of nothingness swept over my mind. I felt like I was falling into a deep engulfing abyss. As the sensation consumed me I no longer fought it but embraced the deep nothingness.

Thursday morning my thoughts were numb. I no longer wanted to go out or see anyone. My only notion was sleep and with that sleep would come the sweet release from the pain of life. I longed for the nothingness. I longed for the black cloak to return to shroud me. I ached for the feeling of complete wholeness granted me by my surrender. A terrifying thought crossed my mind. What if it didn't come back? What if it didn't want me? But somewhere in the back of my mind I recall it promising me it would come back but how do I know it will? How can I trust it to return to me? Lies exist everywhere like the plague corrupting innocent and guilty. Lies manifest and grow like cancerous sores consuming all they touch and destroying hopes and fears leaving a deep hole where nothing grows. I did not want this nothingness. I loathed it but at the same time I needed it because there was nothing else left for me. I had still not eaten anything and those pills prescribed by the doctor made me feel queasy. Two minutes in a doctor's surgery and they know your state of mind? I did not tell the doctor about the green mist, sleepless nights and my thoughts of escaping it all. Didn't see the point, the surgery was full and I wanted to get home. But I tell you now my dear friend.

Thursday evening came and I seemed to awake as the night grew stronger. Shadows seemed to reach out to me welcoming me to their world and I thought how different everything looked draped in grey. I anticipated the night ahead as a strange ancient longing awoke in me. I closed my eyes and waited. Again the green mist started penetrating through my window, creeping towards me and I welcomed the sweet decaying smell into my senses. I felt the face staring at me but this time it was clearer and for a fleeting moment I seemed to recognise it. I began to let go slowly. Images of friends and family flashed through my mind. I recalled episodes of my life, which seemed so dramatic at the time but now seem trivial grains of sand. I let myself float into the nothingness. I imagined myself moving quickly now escaping this mortal life and energising my soul into a collective power. The oppressive cloak had shrouded me and the pain was numbing slowly. Then I was suddenly afraid, I wanted to wake. Monstrous images were flashing through my mind again. This was not right, I did not belong to this distant world that was calling me with its demonic voices. The familiar face seemed to be willing me to wake and open my eyes, but I could not. I drifted into nothingness and embraced the calm awareness of peace.

I awoke at dawn. I tried to call but your phone was off. I now know what I have to do. They will tell you I took my own life but you will know the truth. You will know about the green mist and you will know that the blood that gushed out of my veins did not flow freely, but was led out by an ancient collective presence. There are legions of us being consumed by nothingness. Escaping from the harsh realities of feeling and pain into a blissful, peaceful nothingness. We are all part of that primeval collective race. You will know that I have escaped to a better world. A world where there are no feelings, only beautiful numbness. Most importantly I want you to know that I now know whom the face belonged to. It was I. A distant memory of who I once was before life sapped me of my pleasures, hopes and energies. Before I was engulfed in a life of an all-consuming cloak of grey, oppressive nothingness. The pain I was feeling was a last glimpse of myself trying to regain my emotions, but I am beyond redemption. I have succumbed to the nothingness and I do not deserve to live amongst the mortal emotional beings that plague this world hoping for love. The pain of life is too severe, it has to be extinguished. I hope you will understand now how I will give in to that sweet surrender and to that other world of nothingness ...

DAVID
Steve Hurst

David knew today was special, the secret phone calls and building tension between his parents told him so. His mother was fussing over him while dressing him in his best clothes.

'Don't get dirty David,' she kept telling him as he sat on the floor playing with his Winnie the Pooh jigsaw. His father was acting strangely too, prowling up and down the hallway and staring at the telephone as if daring it to ring. Never mind, he was going to Grandma's, he loved his grandma, she was special. David stayed at Grandma's house more than his own. His largely absent parents had delegated the upbringing of their only child to Grandma and she was the one who held him close, hugged him and made him feel safe.

The Nelsons arrived at Grandma's house to find it full of activity. David was ushered into the summerhouse while his parents joined the main party and he sat down on the floor to play with his cars. After a while he became bored of being alone and decided to join the grown-ups in the main house. David left the summerhouse and listened outside the door to the party inside, it sounded very exciting. After a few minutes someone heard his polite knocking on the door and let him in. He entered the lounge and made his way through a sea of legs towards his mother, his young ears attuned to her voice. He found her over by the big table chatting and drinking with some grown-ups. David tugged at her skirt for attention. Diane Nelson, somewhat tipsy from the flowing wine, squatted down unsteadily at face level with her son.

'Do you want to see Grandma now, David?'

'Yes, yes, Grandma,' he replied and Diane picked him up to look down into the long wooden box on the table.

David peered at the white frail corpse of his dead grandmother, lying amidst purple satin dressed in her best clothes and jewellery. He reached out and touched her dry skin. It was cold and held no life. Her lifeless eyes stared upwards as he poked the eyelids. His mother slurred, 'Doesn't she look peaceful, she's gone to Heaven David, she's in Heaven now.'

David didn't think she looked peaceful at all, and the corpse didn't smell like Grandma. David touched its hand and felt a sudden spark shoot up his arms, jolting his insides. 'That's not Grandma,' he announced and wriggled to be allowed back down onto the floor. His mother unsteadily put him back down on his feet and he worked his way back through the sea of legs to his toys in the summerhouse. Something had happened to Grandma.

That night, after being put to bed he sneaked back into the dark quiet house, into Grandma's kitchen and looked in the pantry. He found the flour and covered his face and hands with it before returning to his bed in the summerhouse. He lay on top of the covers, freezing cold, staring at the ceiling, willing himself to join Grandma in Heaven.

The death affected the Nelsons in different ways. Derrick Nelson used some of the inheritance to fund his son's private education and some to pay for increasingly extravagant business trips abroad. Diane Nelson became even more isolated and sought solace in her growing alcohol addiction, while David gleaned his only affection in tear ridden drunken embraces from his mother during his rare visits home. Withdrawn and devoid of emotional support he proved an easy target during his first year at public school.

'It will toughen the boy up,' his father frequently declared to his despairing lonely mother, but this was no comfort to David. Diane Nelson didn't drive; which was probably a good thing in her condition; so she relied on a dwindling number of friends and distant relatives to take her on school visits. Derrick was always too busy.

When the end of his first year finally arrived, David couldn't wait to leave his place of torment and eagerly awaited the arrival of his father's car crunching up the long gravel school drive. Other children were rushing round excitedly, laden with books and sports equipment, being picked up and swung around by equally excited parents. His father's car came to a halt by the steps opposite the school's main entrance and David rushed through the entrance hall to greet him. As he pushed through the log jam by the main door he watched in horror as his father tapped another boy on the shoulder and then picked him up in his arms in a welcoming embrace. David stood stunned, watching, unbelieving, tears streaming down his face as his father slowly realised it wasn't his son he was holding and carefully placed the bemused boy back on the ground. This wasn't the joyful reunion David had eagerly anticipated, but it did assist in the toughening up process.

The following years could easily have been filled with further misery and isolation, but David slowly adapted and built a defensive shell around his emotions, gradually warming to his surroundings. The strict conformity of public school life suited his perfectionist attitude and he grew stronger and more resilient.

Adults, he learnt, invariably had character flaws begging to be exploited and generally proved to be gullible and easy to manipulate. His contemporaries, however, were harder to understand and his methods of dealing with them were different. A small incident involving a fellow pupil's hand, pinned to a woodwork bench with a bradawl had succeeded in securing a certain respect for David, sufficient to prevent the practical jokes against him from getting out of hand.

The celebration of David's tenth birthday was coming to a close. His friends from the dorm had run through a succession of pranks guaranteed to amuse, but not overly offend and now he lay on his back listening to the last whispers fade away in the cold dark dormitory. The long heavy curtains muffled the outside world and he fell asleep, content with his surroundings. Suddenly, he was wide awake, there was something in the dorm, he could sense it near the foot of his bed. As adrenaline pumped through him, he opened his eyes and stared straight into the face of a beast, impossible but it was there, glaring down at him with red hypnotic eyes, full of malice. Terrified, he couldn't look away, the creature seemed to hypnotise him, he couldn't move. Dave could just make out the shape of a half-beast, half-man, glowing red from a source within, while the eyes held him captive. David silently begged for others in the dorm to wake up, take the demon's attention, and let him escape while it ripped them apart, but they didn't. Time seemed frozen; nothing existed but David and the demon as it looked into his soul, communicating with him in a way he didn't understand. David lay paralysed, defenceless, awaiting his destruction. The beast would take him now, crush him and toss him aside. It didn't, it rummaged through David's soul, collected what it wanted, changed what it didn't like, then it was gone.

He knew it had gone, time was returning to normal and he could hear himself breathing. He remained rigid, not moving for another hour before he felt it was safe to look. He lay there awake for the rest of the night paralysed with fear.

Over the next few days David searched for a credible solution to the demon's appearance. He closely questioned his fellow pupils from the dormitory, but nobody seemed to understand or be hiding anything. The demon didn't return and he gradually filed the incident away in a memory domain rarely consciously visited, but never forgotten.

During the remaining years of his incarceration at the school David grew in intelligence, strength and power. He could have been a leader, but chose instead to allow those around him to underestimate his capabilities. Occasionally a bizarre act of cruelty would give the others an insight into his character and a warning to keep their distance, but his general aim was to remain anonymous, his time would come.

On his graduation, both parents were forced to take time out of their lives and attend the ceremony. He felt like an actor playing a role, he had gradually become aware of his capacity to interact with others, whilst feeling he was watching from the outside. He observed his parents struggling out of their comfort zone, and was amused by it. Things were going to be different when he returned home. After a meaningless ceremony and tedious goodbyes, the Nelsons finally departed.

David sat in the back seat of his father's luxury car partly listening to the conversation offered. His mother annoyed him intensely by now, constantly drivelling on about matters of no possible importance. She seemed incapable of keeping her boring menial thoughts to herself, droning on relentlessly about nothing. His father was attempting to plan David's future, one that would keep David out of the way and under control, but it seemed he was planning the future of someone else. None of it mattered. David's father had not sufficiently developed an effective method of ignoring his wife's ramblings and the car's speed through the country lanes accelerated with his agitation.

'Mrs Algate's son works in a pharmacy now, he looks really smart and he's ever so polite. Derrick please slow down!' On and on, faster and faster, the car was beginning to slide in the corners. David loved it.

'Have you seen Glynis lately? I'm sure she's put on weight; you'd think she'd change her hair now she's that age, Derrick are you listening? Slow down, you're scaring me!'

The veins were protruding in Derrick's neck, his grip on the wheel causing his hands to turn white. The car was hurtling past trees and ditches; David willed it on faster, faster. He was laughing now, leaning forward between the seats.

Suddenly, the back of a lorry appeared from nowhere, the car's tyres screeched on wet tarmac, losing control then careering off the road, it hit a low grass bank and catapulted into the air. Everything went into slow motion, CDs, pens and other small items floated around the cars interior, no noise, slow chaos. David waited for the impact as the car came down to earth; nose first, smashing into the ground, windows shattering, metal contorting, then silence again.

David kicked open the rear door and emerged almost unscathed, falling out of the mangled black car that lay on its roof some distance below the road. He reached through the broken side window and touched his mother's neck, still alive but unconscious, her face a mass of bloodied flesh pierced by shards of glass. David thought about Glynis' hairstyle problem and moved round to look at his father, crushed against the steering wheel, struggling to breathe, a peculiar rasping sound coming from his bloodied mouth. He moved away, a strong smell of petrol and oil coming from the wreckage, climbed back up the bank and took a crumpled cigarette from its packet, noting how steady his hands were. He sat down and smoked, barely noticing the car, wondering absently how long it would take before somebody came.

Everyone was sympathetic to David at the joint funeral, how very sorry, what a terrible accident. He couldn't wait for everyone to leave; his insincere grief was wearing a bit thin. At least he'd managed to get the police off his back, they had seemed confused, if not quite accusatory with him during one of the interviews he'd endured. The police couldn't understand how both front seat belts had become unattached during the crash, or why David hadn't been injured. David hid behind his false anguish and wondered idly whether his casually discarded cigarette had caused the car to ignite.

No matter, he was wealthy and free of the parents he'd come to despise. His time had come.

THE SÉANCE
A K Still

The note was brief and to the point: A request to hold a séance. I'd earned a good living from my 'gift' for the past five years. My clients were usually satisfied with what I had to tell them, as was I with the £50 fee for the consultation.

The house was just a ten minute walk from my flat. An elderly man answered the door and led me into a room where a woman, strikingly like him, already waited.

'Right, I'm Ted Burns and this is my sister Rose. We want you to contact our dead mum, the evil old bat that she was.' The statement, like the note, was brief and to the point.

The woman winced, but the man simply shrugged. 'I don't believe in all this séance nonsense, but we're desperate and I'll try anything.'

The woman seemed suddenly to take hold of herself. 'Please forgive my brother. I know you from the spiritual church, Mr James.'

I looked puzzled. 'I've never seen you there.'

She smiled, 'You wouldn't, I usually sit right at the back.'

I ignored the angry glare from her brother and addressed the woman. 'So, how can I help?'

'We've lived here all our lives, neither of us married. We're twins and we were ten years old when our mother died; our aunt Amy came to live here with us then.'

'And she was just as evil as our old lady,' snarled Ted Burns.

Rose Burns shook her head before continuing. 'There were a lot of rumours when our mother died. She may have left a lot of money hidden somewhere, but we never found a penny. No one did.'

'Tore this place apart, we did,' said the old man. 'And so did our aunt and others too, over the years.'

'And you want me to hold a séance to find out where this money is hidden?' I said.

'Well that's what you do, ain't it?' he said.

'I try to make contact with past loved ones, Mr Burns,' I answered. 'But it doesn't sound as if your mother was loved.'

Ted angrily passed a piece of crumbled paper to his sister. 'Our mother was responsible for the deaths of at least three young women,' she said.

I gulped. Rose nodded sadly. 'She performed illegal abortions.'

'The police couldn't prove anything,' said Ted. 'They tried, but she was too clever for them.' Rose nodded. 'Then there were the loans. The term loan shark wasn't invented then, but she was a shark all right.'

'When was all this?' I asked.

'Years ago, she died in 1950.'

'That's over fifty years ago,' I said. 'So why now?'

'Money,' said Ted, bluntly. 'We're broke and if our dear old mum did leave a stash, we want it. Aunt Amy never found it, she would have pushed off if she had, but she stayed until she died in 1963.'

'We made our own enquiries but in the end we drew a blank. Then about a month ago this turned up.' Rose passed the piece of crumpled paper back to her brother.

He read it angrily, 'Somewhere in this house is hidden all my money. Money hard earned, ridding careless, dirty girls of their unwanted babies and money lent to, and paid back by, the wives of drunkards that guzzled the housekeeping. No one approved of what I did, but everyone will be after my money. Good luck with the search, but better you learn to do what I did. Those old crochet needles will be a lot easier to find.'

I winced and immediately sympathised with Ted's view of his evil mother. 'Where did you get this?' I asked.

'Found it behind the kitchen sink when the council gave us a new kitchen,' said Ted. 'So, will you help us then?'

'Yes, I'll do what I can,' I answered, excited at the prospect of finding the old woman's hidden money.

The two elderly people led me upstairs to a back bedroom; this was where I should perform the séance. 'This was her bedroom and where she used to do the abortions too,' said Ted. 'Our aunt slept in here when she moved in.'

'It has a bad atmosphere,' I said, going straight into my routine.

Ted shrugged, 'So what do we do now then?'

'We hold hands and pray.'

'She won't recognise any prayer,' said Ted taking my hand.

The moment we held hands an intense coldness filled the room. Rose felt it too and shivered violently.

Aloud, I prayed and requested any spirit that might be present to come forward. Immediately the heavy curtains rose into the air, as though carried on a violent wind. All three of us stared at the closed windows.

Rose Burns fainted, as the wind grew stronger. I ducked as the curtain wires broke, but Ted Burns was too slow and the wire slashed across the cheek. He cried out in pain. 'You spiteful old swine.'

Rose Burns had fallen onto the bed. 'I think we should stop right now,' I said.

Ted Burns shook his head angrily. 'I'm not giving up now and neither are you.' He grabbed my arm with surprising strength.

Argument was pointless, so I tried persuasion. 'But Rose needs to see a doctor.'

'She's only fainted,' he grabbed Rose's hand. 'It's better for her this way.'

I whispered a prayer and spoke again. 'Can you tell us who you are?'

Ted Burns snorted. 'We know who she is. What we want to know is where the evil old swine hid her ill-gotten gains.'

The effect was electric. The light flashed on and exploded.

Ted dropped Rose's hand and looked wildly about. Rose opened her eyes but fainted once more as the bed rose into the air.

Ted grabbed his sister, but the bed crashed down, knocking him unconscious.

A thin mist swirled around the room engulfing me; I shook with fear and intense cold.

The swirling mist, holding me physically in its grasp, hurled me from the room.

Gradually the mist took on the form of an elderly woman. Smiling evilly, she waved her arm and I was hurled down the stairs.

She appeared instantly at my side and dragged me roughly along the passage to the kitchen. Laughing wickedly she hurled me into the backyard.

Somehow I staggered the short distance to my flat. The following morning I awoke with my body covered in cuts and bruises.

I had to find out what had happened to Ted and Rose Burns. I put on a long coat, to hide the worst of my injuries, and hurried to the Burns' house.

The street was cordoned off. Police cars, an ambulance and an undertaker's van stood inside the cordoned area.

Onlookers stood idly around talking about what had happened. As one of the bystanders left the group I nodded towards the Burns' house. 'What's happened down there?' I asked.

The man glanced only briefed at my bruised face. 'Two old people have been topped. They just bought them out in those temporary coffins they use.'

'Blimey,' I said, trying not to sound too concerned.

'Yeah, terrible,' he said. 'Some kind of black magic nonsense they reckon. They ought to string them up when they catch them, that's what I reckon.'

'Yeah, too right they should,' I gulped.

ZOMBIE
Fred Brown

I'm a zombie, I thought.

This was an entirely new state of being for me, but in that original lucid moment, I could not remember what I had been before, although there was a void in my mind, which I knew had once contained some other experience. I was quite sure I had not been a zombie before. I was not unhappy about being a zombie: far from it. In fact, I felt something like relief. And quiet satisfaction. It seemed a suitably bad thing to me.

As I thought this first thought, and entertained these emotions, I was shuffling along a street, with purpose. I had no idea what the purpose was, although I felt the street was familiar. Just ahead of me was a large, dark, malevolent building, which I knew was a church. It felt like coming home to go into it; an awesome, uncomfortable feeling. Somebody ran in before me, and I had my second thought.

That's the driver.

I was certain I had been in some sort of contact with this driver before, and very recently. It was urgent that I saw him. So I shuffled into the church. It was dark and draughty, very comfortable. I had no difficulty at all in seeing him, now that the street lamps were not hurting my eyes and blurring everything. The driver was huddled among the pews. I smashed right through them, as if I was walking through waves. It was something I realised I could not have done minutes before. I felt strong and glorious as the wood snapped around my legs, so I knocked a few holes out with my hands as well. The driver suddenly screamed and jumped straight through a window which collapsed in a glory of disintegrating colours.

I felt very contented as I walked through the wall of the church and down the street. I almost remembered making some sort of contented sounds in my life before this, and twisted my mouth into different shapes by instinct until a satisfying growl emerged. I shuffled and growled my way along the street, paying no attention to anyone, and receiving no attention from them, until I met a few people I at first took to be fellow zombies. They were all bald-headed, and were writing Skinz on a wall with aerosol paint. When they saw me they contemplated me for a moment. Then the biggest of them spoke.

'What you gawpin' at, uh?'

A second one attracted some attention by spitting into my eye. The spittle caressed my cheek in a most pleasant manner.

'Ey, Body,' sneered the Expectorator, 'Za Nig. Lez bust 'im. Uh.'

Body ruminated on his gum.

'Giz niff, Ox,' he snarled at last.

Ox waddled across and passed the glue bag to him. Body had a long and apparently satisfying sniff. Ox received the bag again and sniffed with no less pleasure, and the Expectorator expectorated from deep in his throat and sniffed longer than any of them. They all stared at me with joyful sullenness and, having satisfied themselves with my appearance, and expressed concern at my absence from home, they advanced slowly, though not entirely in a straight line. Body hit me in the face and the blow felt quite soft. Quite enjoyable, in fact. That surprised me. But now, I reflected, that I was a zombie, a whole new range of experiences and sensations awaited my exploration. As well as the purely tactile pleasure of the blow I experienced a sudden hunger, and bit his hand. Never had I tasted anything as good as this mixture of warm, sweet blood, chewy muscle and crunchable bone. Body yelled after a moment, 'Look at me and. Zbit me 'and off!'

Ox bellowed and squared up to me. I interpreted his words as, 'Bitz and. Ya don't do that frienda mine!'

He headbutted me and again I felt delightfully surprised by the remarkably soft, even delicate, effect. And I was still hungry. His nose was temptingly close, and I bit it. It tasted even better than Body's hand, a truly delectable dessert. They both ran away. Although I was disappointed that the feast was thus removed from me I felt that it would be inappropriate for a zombie to run, and lumbered on in a dignified style.

I wandered along the streets, quietly enjoying myself, when a car passed. Several cars had, of course, passed me during this time, but this particular car awakened a feeling from my pre-zombie existence which justified my thinking of it as 'the car'. The people in it were also known to be by the same kind of déjà-vu. However, at the very moment that a thought on the subject was about to formulate itself, I felt myself leaving my body. I enjoyed the body I had, and felt emotionally attached to it, so I used all the energy I could muster to retain it, and I felt hungry again. In particular, I felt hungry for the contents of the car. I believed that I had a right to gorge myself on them. The others who still wandered round the streets did not whet my appetite in the least, though I did notice that I licked my lips every time I passed one of them.

Suddenly an idea emerged, quite spontaneously. I knew that if I waited where I was, the car would return. My déjà-vu was strong. I had been hit before, at this very spot, by this very car, driven by these very people. So I waited, and was very content. Night passed, day came, night returned - oh I don't know how many times, until, at last, sure enough, the car came, driven as if by madmen. I stood where I was, and they knocked me down.

I heard the voice of a young man in panic.

'F**k's sake, Pete, this is the second one in a week!'

A second and similar voice added, 'You'll be done if you don't watch it, Pete.'

Hands, which I felt sure were Pete's felt me, lager fumes which I imagined was the breath of Pete wafted over me, and a voice which I assumed belonged to Pete asked, 'Is he dead? Phil, do you think he's dead?'

Phil knelt beside me and felt in the wrong place for my pulse. 'I think he's dead. What do you think, John?' He poured a little lager over me.

John kicked me casually. ''e's dead.'

Pete heaved a sigh and said, with enormous relief, 'That's all right then. He won't be able to shop me.'

'You can't go killing peds like that though,' grumbled John. 'Tain't right.'

'Aw, forget it. There's nowt we can do now,' yawned Phil, with finality. 'Come on.'

John put his hand near my face and I bit it. He yelled, naturally, while I got up and hit Phil.

Pete began to shout. 'Now just hold on. You should watch where you're going, you should. You'll get yourself killed.'

Something in my look silenced him.

''e's nearly bit me 'and off!' said John. 'I'm gonna bloody kill 'im!'

'He's the one! Remember my dream? Well it wasn't. It was him!'

'You're p****d,' snapped Phil. 'It was a dream, but what he's going to get isn't.'

'He's got phenomenal strength,' stammered Pete. 'He broke the pews like balsa wood.'

I couldn't speak, of course, but I agreed with him by pulling a nearby shrub out of the ground and kicking a statue over. I did both in such a way that I herded them against a wall.

'Start praying, Pete,' blubbered John. 'You can bloody pray, can't you? Start praying then.'

But instead Pete darted to my left. As I moved to intercept him the others did likewise to my right, and in the confusion they all got into the car and started it. This was no problem. I stood in front of it, lifted it and tossed it over onto its back, where it buzzed like an insect with a sudden loss of dignity. The occupants added to the pleasure of the occasion by screaming and yelling at the tops of their voices. I grabbed Pete by the hair and pulled him out, and was just about to bite his head off when my body fell off. This was dreadfully annoying.

I was, I feel, rather fortunate in finding this new body, which was sitting at this very typewriter when the person within it terminated occupation. I have drunk his whisky, which could be much improved by the addition of a generous infusion of blood, and was much struck by the final sentence of his composition: She whimpered like a puppy as my hand passed over the sheer silk and stroked her warm, soft, naked thigh.

My purpose in writing these few notes is this. Many of you who may read this are likely to become zombies. I feel that I can do my bit to reassure you about this mode of existence, the idea of which, I seem to remember, fills the ordinary human being with loathing and disgust. I trust that this little account of my experiences will endear us to you.

I can almost taste that thigh.

THE OPEN DOOR
John J Allan

The cottage stood in a plot of land on the edge of the village. It was a pretty cottage. One could almost say it was a classic cottage; a picture postcard cottage. Thatched and beamed in Tudor times it had been unoccupied for many years and was showing signs of neglect. It was surrounded by what had been a pretty country garden. Now sadly overgrown, the more robust plants struggling to break through the weeds, to bloom in a desultory way. The rustic arch on which clung the remnants of a rambling rose on the verge of collapse.

To us children it was the source off much mystery and speculation, standing as it did, empty and shuttered. An open invitation, for the front door was always half open. One thing stopped us children who usually rampaged through any barn or ruined building that we came across. Why did this one not suffer the same fate? *Because it was haunted!*

Everyone said so. Everyone knew it was.

'You know what happened there?'

'Terrible going's on.'

'I've seen lights at night.'

'Movements at the upstairs windows.'

'Wouldn't go in there if you paid me.'

So the comments went on, repeated and embroidered. It was not surprising that we children were affected. In fact, in the winter when it was dark we would go round the long way, down Long Barrow Walk, rather than pass the 'Haunted House'.

As I grew older, I became known as a daredevil. Somebody had only to say, 'I bet you won't do that,' for me to immediately do it. 'I bet you won't walk across the weir.' Green, slimy and incredibly slippery. I did it! 'I bet you won't jump off that high wall.' I did it! Hurting my ankle but not letting on. 'I bet you won't walk along the roof.' Balancing on the ridge tiles of Cartwright's barn, forty feet above the ground. I did it!

I became quite a hero until one day Peggy Masters, who I had a crush on, said, 'I bet you won't go in the haunted house.' I was surrounded by eager faces, expectant faces. All waiting for my decision, to pick up the gauntlet that had been thrown down. They all sensed the hesitation, the reluctance, the fear, and one by one they began to jeer.

'Windy, windy, cowardly, cowardly custard, we dare you. Dare, dare.' The words rang out louder and louder. There in the crowd was Peggy. Smiling, pretty, smug. I started to hate her. How could she do this to me? Me who loved her so much. My reputation was at stake.

I opened the gate, which creaked ominously, and struggled slowly through the overgrown path, up the steps until I stood by the open door. I looked back at the awe-struck group of children, their faces anticipating my next move. As I hesitated a solitary and strangled cry rang out, 'Windy.' The dye was cast, I'd come this far, there was no retreat. I pushed through the half open door and stood inside. It took a few seconds for my eyes to get used to the gloom. As the mist started to clear, a quiet voice made me jump. 'Come in young man.' It was a sweet, friendly voice, a woman's voice. I walked through a door into a charming room. Bright and airy, it was bedecked with fresh flowers. White lace curtains blew in the warm breeze revealing a view of a pretty, well tended garden. White antimacassars and doilies adorned everywhere. Highly polished antique furniture stood around, the walls covered in photographs in sparkling silver frames together with ornaments and knick-knacks. Pictures of highland cattle standing in moorland streams adorned the walls. By the window on a floral settee sat two white-haired old ladies, while just behind them stood a grim-faced elderly gentleman with a large flowing moustache.

'Come in my dear,' said the taller of the two ladies. 'I am Elsie Morgan and this lady is my sister Muriel and the gentleman is our brother Reginald. And what is your name?'

'Ben,' I croaked, my dry throat making speech difficult.

'Please don't be nervous. Come and sit here. We've been expecting you.' I sat where she pointed on a high-backed chair. 'Do you like buns?' she enquired, 'sticky buns?'

'Yes,' I said eagerly, this time the words came out more easily.

'I expect you would like some lemonade too? I made some fresh this morning,' said the other older lady. 'Don't mind if our brother doesn't say much. He's a little ...' here she tapped her forehead significantly. I relaxed for I was warming to these friendly old ladies.

'Do you live in the village?' enquired Elsie, giving me a sweet smile.

'Yes,' I said, 'I live at the other end with my mum and dad, he's Joe Cheeseman, the blacksmith,' I volunteered. 'Oh and there is my sister Lucy, but she is only five.'

'Well,' said Elsie, giving me a great big smile. 'That sounds like a lovely family.'

Suddenly the big man spoke, his face contorting, 'One day I'm going to kill you both.'

'Oh … you do get some funny ideas Reggie,' said Elsie dismissing this outburst. 'Take no notice,' she said to me once more tapping her forehead and giving me a knowing look.

Quite suddenly, I knew I had to get away. Get away quickly from this strange and unreal trio. 'I must be going, my friends will be wondering what's happened to me,' I said.

'Do come and visit us again won't you Ben,' insisted Muriel.

'Yes I will, thank you for the bun and lemonade,' I shouted over my shoulder.

As I reached the door I heard terrible screams and looking back over my shoulder saw the man standing over the two old ladies, a large axe raised high above his head. I ran terrified out through the front door and found myself on the overgrown garden path. It was growing dark and there at the gate I was confronted by a crowd of wide-eyed villagers and friends. Bob, the village policeman was advancing towards me. 'What have you been doing in there all this time, lad? You've been in there for hours and all those terrible noises.'

'What noises?' I said, 'I only had a glass of lemonade and a bun with two old ladies and a gentleman,' I protested.

'The Morgans,' I heard someone in the crowd whisper. 'Oh my god, they've been dead this five and thirty years!'

A gasp of horror rose from the crowd. 'They were ever so nice,' I shouted. 'Look here, they gave me another bun as I was leaving,' I said holding it up. It was indeed a sticky bun and it was splattered in fresh blood.

THE STRANGER
Lucy Rushen

The day of Friday the 13th, is it superstition or is it bad luck or both? This is a day I never wanted to remember as long as I lived, as the only memory of a close friend is never going to become reality again. My true best friend dying right in front of my eyes is something never to be witnessed again, by me in anyway at all. This feeling felt like a heart attack beating at the head and heart, my soul crying a river of the memories that have been shared. The tears not being cried have been all cried out. The telling of people who don't know what my heartache feels, losing the friend who was more of a sister to me. I had been blamed for the murder of my friend by her parents.

Brooke, my best friend, at the time, was 15 years old and had blondish brown hair and blue sparkling eyes. Me, being known as Jaycee, was the same age, had brown hair and dull brown eyes.

The evening began with a bang, going out clubbing in Sound nightclub in London's Leicester Square. Everything was fine, but a figure that I thought was following us, tracked us down to the club only to find out Brooke dropped her purse out of her bag. We both carried ID of our ages, money to get in and mobiles for emergencies. This strange figure was a young male 20-30 years old and had a very distinctive smell, it was some sort of very expensive aftershave and had a tattoo on his left shoulder of a black panther.

The night was young and so were we, filling the evening with flirting and rejections, the future not to be tampered with, but only we alone spending the Friday night on the tiles. Brooke felt slightly weird in someway (I always thought she was telepathic or even psychic) she sensed a bad feeling, and wasn't wrong there. As we were walking down the street at 12am, the wind was slapping us in the face, heels on our ankle-breaking shoes were clicking loudly on the cold pavement below. Our frozen feet and our skirts were a bit too short to keep us even the slightest bit warm. It was extremely scary as too many long, thin shadowed silhouettes looked like they were edging towards us underneath the street lamps in the street.

Brooke was linked onto a really gorgeous looking guy who had blond hair and blue eyes, 5ft 7in and slim, muscled build, 16 years old. I got lumbered with a brown haired, green-eyed guy about 5ft 5in, bit short for me, quite slim and kind of cute. I couldn't care less, it was just a bit of fun, you know a quick kiss in a public area, get their mobile numbers then ditch them before they ditch you. I got to the point where I was worried that Brooke and I were slowly losing time to get home before all buses stopped routing for the night. I was shouting to Brooke and she stopped what was she doing, probably something rude, hey I never did find out! She said her longest goodbye to him, which was to kiss him so much he had no lips left on his poor little handsome face. I had already told Richie that it was like a one-night stand but no funny business, just purely kiss each other's faces off. Brooke didn't finish with hers, although he lives in Welling and she lives in Lewisham. The number, 07763 ... and his name, Connor, was stored automatically on her phone, she didn't want to break his little heart so she stayed with him out of kindness.

We stumbled back through the streets of London, back to the bus garage when a strange figure appeared from nowhere and grabbed us. This man was dressed in a balaclava and wearing all black. He tried so hard to drag us to a sealed area where no one could see what was happening. Appearing from a dark, dirty back alleyway was another man, some friend of the one that grabbed us; he grabbed me and put his filthy hand over my mouth and the other hand round my waist. He pulled a long, grubby rope out from his bag and bound my hands together, another rope was placed round my delicate, cold ankles. As he threw me to the ground he told me to stay silent and stay where I was or I would be next.

Brooke didn't know what to do, she was so scared she was crying and screaming. A hand suddenly was put over her mouth, this man was telling her to shut up. I watched what happened, he bound her hands to a fence and placed a piece of tape over her mouth. I could see Brooke's eyes, they looked heavy, and the sparkle was lost, her only chance of staying celibate to Connor was if she still had her innocence, she looked uncomfortable and I knew that what just happened to her was going to happen to me. I was being held in an awkward position, a piece of tape was placed over my mouth and a knife was placed at my throat, I knew now something bad was going to happen to me. The darkened man picked up my feet and pulled them so I was lying on my back, my back was hurting, my hands were bound behind me, he was pushing my skirt up and ... I'm not going to tell the rest, you know what happened, I got raped. I saw blood pouring from my wrists, pouring from my legs and trickling down my left arm, the man was bad enough to leave me with a few cuts, which looked deliberate.

The next thing I knew I heard a gun shot, my eyes went blurry, I saw a pool of thickened red blood. I saw the knife on the floor next to her covered in blood, my blood, Brooke's blood. I saw my best friend lying on her stomach, head bleeding and stomach bleeding. I think she was stabbed in her stomach and shot in her head. The two men ran off as soon as the damage was done, leaving evidence behind. I remember trying to shuffle over to her, I picked up the knife and started cutting away at the rope round my hands. I felt the knife cutting and once the rope was cut, I felt the blade cut the side of my wrist. I cut away the ones round my feet and stumbled along the path to Brooke, she was really bad, I checked her pulse but it was negative. I tried to find my phone, I searched over the place for my bag and I saw the handles. Brooke was lying on my bag. I picked up her bag and found her phone, I phone an ambulance and phoned the police.

Flashes of blue shot down the road at us. Paramedics checked Brooke. They shook their heads and I collapsed on the floor in tears, I was shocked and upset that she had gone. The police tried to take a statement, they got nothing. I sat slumped in the corner, tears rolling down from my eyes, I couldn't move. I was helped into the ambulance, my injuries were treated on the way to the hospital, I was crying hysterically. I phoned Brooke's parents; they blamed me for her death, her mother said from the start never to trust a spoilt girl like me. That was what made me worst, I phoned my parents, and they were saying things like: Are you alright? Is Brooke alright? What happened? OK we will be there in a minute. Just stay there.

Brooke's parents arrived first; I said I was very sorry and that I wished it never happened at all. Her father said he would have been happier if it was me lying there as stiff as a rock. I ran out of the room, they put me into a state of guilt. I felt helpless for trying to help her. I was praying so much that I wished it had never happened. For the hour I was waiting for my parents I only confided in one person who really understood me, that person was God. He knew my pain; He knew what it was like to lose a person. Well at least Brooke was away from harm's danger (she probably even grew a decent pair of angel's wings and a halo that wouldn't fall off if she was bad).

My parents finally turned up, I had been sitting outside in the pouring rain for them, my mum thought she had better get me inside to see a doctor in case I had got hypothermia. I had a high temperature, I was shivering and my skin was burning up pretty bad. I pulled off every dressing covering my wounds, I exposed them to infection and was sitting there scratching them to make them bleed. My dad came up to me, picked me up and walked into the hospital. My wounds were cleaned up and dressed again.

The police asked me more questions about the murder of Brooke Paige, my best friend (in case you forgot), questions about the men, what weapons did they have? What were they wearing? The stupid questions were the ones I already thought I had answered earlier in that day. All I said was that the men were tall, dark skinned or maybe half-cast.

I returned home after a couple of days in the hospital and I wasn't feeling hungry, although I really was, I didn't have enough energy to make it into my room so I was carried to my room. There were too many pictures of us pulling silly faces. I had sleepless nights for the next two to three weeks. I even arrived at Brooke's funeral in a wheelchair as my whole body went completely limp.

I remembered Connor, the lover of the evening that Brooke picked up. I rang him and asked him to come down for the funeral, but he refused to see her in her coffin. The phrase he used was 'I don't want to remember my girlfriend in a wooden box being carried down a path to be viewed by everyone'. I must admit he was crying on the phone and I sent him a photo of her posing on the swings in the local park. Connor and I still talk. I've met him several times since Brooke's funeral and I've even caught him sleeping by her grave so he can be close to her.

I was sent to a rehab centre because my parents caught me cutting up my arms. I would sit in the corner of my room looking up at photos of us while running a blade up my arms. I didn't care if the blade was dirty or even covered in disease, I just wanted to leave the world and join my best friend in Heaven. That's what her parents would have wanted me to do, kill myself to make them feel better. If time could be reversed they would change the fact, it would be me dead. They would do anything to get their daughter back in their lives. I spent six months recovering from my ordeal, I even spent thousands of pounds on a psychiatrist. The time I spent off school was about a year. I got back and everyone wanted to be my new best friend. Some girls even got jealous of me being friends with Brooke and tried dressing like her to get recognition.

Ever since she left me without saying goodbye, I know in my heart that she wanted to go with everyone's interests at heart and she is constantly saying sorry to everyone she has hurt in the past. I visit her grave every day to tell her what has happened at school, at the weekend or wherever I am.

Brooke, my best friend, I will never forget the day you left the world a way all parents have feared. It's not your fault you lost your life; it's not your fault that everyone is hurt by it and it's not your fault, it was your life taken. You went with the slightest bit of pain. Whatever you do, never stop believing in yourself.

WALKING WITH DEATH
Sue Round

She is destined to walk in the man's shadow. Compelled to share his anger ... his thoughts ... but worst of all she must share his wickedness.

He stole her life ... swept it away with just two strokes of his glinting hand. She needs revenge ... needs to find peace. Until that time she is bound by invisible ropes and must share his every move.

He, the demon who violated her body ... the butcher who inflicted such horrific pain is her gaoler. The keeper of her soul.

If only she'd had the pittance, the mere four pennies to pay for lodgings, then she wouldn't have been forced to walk the dark streets. Wouldn't have met the fiend who hates and preys on women.

* * *

In the darkness before dawn she is with him ... close by his side as he lures another young woman to her death. Into an empty yard they go, hidden from prying eyes he pounces.

She sees things no living mortal ought ever to see. Her mind shrieks in silent horror. No words leave her lips as she desperately tries to warn the girl.

'Annie,' (she hears the girl's name) '*Annie go back ... go now,*' she cries.

But words do not leave her empty mouth.

All *she* can do is watch ... is feel ... close her eyes in terror as his adept hand slashes again and again. His blows almost sever the girl's head. Through tight-closed lids *she* sees it all ... compelled by her binding to watch.

His shimmering blade slides slowly down Annie's body, leaving a crimson snake-trail in its wake. *She* feels the heat as vacuous steam rises from the warm cavity.

With trembling hands he rips apart the reddening skin to reveal the innards which, once lay content beside Annie's beating heart. *She* must witness the vile act as he raises the coils of throbbing life. *She* lets out a silent scream as he severs and places them gently onto Annie's rapidly cooling shoulder.

He stares down at his handiwork and smiles.

'*Thank the Lord that Annie is finally dead,*' she prays.

One final act and his terrible night's work is done. Swiftly, with the ease of a butcher ... the knowledge of a surgeon, he removes the triangular organ that is the symbol of womanhood, and places it in his secret pouch.

* * *

Three weeks go by ... three peaceful weeks during which he hasn't gone out again. *She* is grateful for the respite ... even praying that her ordeal is over.

She is wrong.

Again he finds a likely victim. *She* feels the hatred inside him. Once more he is sweet-talking ... once again he is dancing a woman to her death.

This victim is almost as tall as him. She allows herself to be led ... allows his strong hands to take her into the deserted alleyway. This girl even smiles up at him as he draws close.

'Beware,' she cries. 'Beware the knife.'

But his victim doesn't listen ... she cannot hear the silent warning. She gives herself to him completely.

Twice the flashing blade slides across her neck ... twice his victim tries to scream. Only to be thwarted and choke on her own pumping blood.

At last the girl's limp body slumps to the ground. His body stiffens and his head jerks upward. His living ears detect some sound that she cannot. In an instant they are gone ... gaoler and prisoner secreted in the shadows. Only the poor dead victim lies waiting for discovery.

He waits ... he watches ... he listens to the sounds of the night. Muttered words of contempt bounce around the walls of his hiding place. His anger shifts and flies with the breeze. *She knows he is not satisfied ... knows that he will want more. She knows too that his dastardly night's work is not yet over.*

Then, along she comes, another fly walking into his silken spider's trap.

He makes his move. *She recognises the victim ... knows her well ... a sister of the oldest profession.* Desperately she calls out a warning ... a warning, which is never heard.

'Cathy ... Cathy, watch out.'

Her silent warnings are no help to Cathy. He moves in for the kill.

Cathy fights hard against her attacker. She struggles right up to the last moment ... until he makes his final cut.

She feels his rage ... can see it by the way he wields the blade. And *she* knows his terrible thirst for blood will not be quenched until he has taken from Cathy the parts of her body that he desires most.

His accomplished hands move quickly. When finally he is done ... when his anger is spent, he wipes the knife on a fragment of Cathy's apron. Only to toss it away a few seconds later in disgust.

Cathy ... poor Cathy is no more. Another sacrifice to whatever demon he serves.

*   *   *

One week later he is on the prowl again. Seeking another likely victim.

He locates a lone woman, who despite all the warnings has found it necessary to walk the lonely streets to earn her money.

His victim is a pretty young thing, catching his lustful eye quickly. Her blonde curls dance seductively with every step. Sparkling blue eyes lure him towards her.

He has no need to tempt ... no need to charm, for she approaches him. Dressed in his great coat and Derby hat, he looks every inch the gentleman.

If only the girl knew ... knew about those pockets ... those deep, deep pockets that hide the tools and keep warm the trophies of his devilish trade.

This woman shows no suspicion ... no fear, as she invites him to her room. Slowly they walk to a place the woman knows well. And *she* is forced to dog their footsteps.

Within the confined space of the back room his victim's screams echo and bounce around the walls. Not until his crazy sport is over does she lay silent and still.

This time there is no need for haste. No fear of discovery. No one to disturb him. He has all the time he needs to fulfil his demonic task.

Methodically he takes the girl's body apart. Beginning with her face, he slices and carves ... a sculptor creating his own masterpiece ... discarding what displeases him.

He works with patience and pleasure. Cutting ... slicing ... rejecting ... tossing pieces of flesh and unwanted organs around the room.

The sight and stench repulses her. Such a sight she has never seen before. But she is unable to look away. She feels each cut … she shudders as his slender fingers reach inside the victim … reach inside her, as he touches and withdraws. She is sickened by the whole experience.

Just when *she* thinks she can take no more, he stops … he is done. Tenderly, almost reverently he lifts and places the victim's heart into his waiting 'poachers' pocket.

He is at last ready to leave the scene of carnage.

*   *   *

As the days pass he becomes quieter … withdrawn, as though his life's work is coming to an end. *She believes he is making peace with himself.* But so much has gone before that she cannot be certain.

She prays that the abominable degradation that is part of her curse is coming to an end. She longs more than anything for her link with him to finally come to a stop … that freedom will soon be hers.

The moon is full as he sets out on the eve of Christmas. He wears no great coat … no Derby hat. His bloodstained tools are secreted in a cupboard.

She accompanies him willingly on this journey. Some inner-sense telling her it will be for the last time.

Through the near-silent streets he walks. *She follows, losing her bearings.* Only the familiar smell of the river comforts *her.* Another twist … another turn and she hears the great bell of the Mother Church. He seems not to hear it. Only one objective seems to occupy his mind.

He stops by the bridge and looks down into the fast flowing water. *She sees the inky-black liquid shimmer in the moonlight.* The water seems to draw *her* … to bring comfort to her troubled mind.

The gentle arms of slumbering blackness pull him close. Encircling him … covering him … dragging him down into the depths.

She feels the pull … feels the loosening of chains … feels the hold he has over her slacken. At last she is free of her gaoler … free of the instrument of Satan. Peace and blissful happiness wash over her.

His time has come. *Her* time has come. They drift apart. He towards the murky bottom of the river. *She* to meet the spirits of her sisters in death.

She is free at last ... she is at peace ... is drifting away from the demon who took her life. Far away from the fiend who forced her to witness despicable acts of torture and death time and time again.

She is free of the man the world will come to know as ...

... Jack The Ripper.

BABY TEETH
Celia Jackson

I was at the vets when I first met them. My old cat was having her regular check-up. She was sitting in her cat basket, her back to me, every line of her body expressing disgust and outrage. The heavy door to the surgery was pushed open and a young woman holding a small boy by one hand and a tiny golden Labrador puppy in the other, backed into the room. I jumped up and held the door for her. She sat down next to me and we introduced ourselves. Her name was Melissa Harris and she said they had moved into the little cottage at the end of my road a few months earlier. She was a pretty girl, slim with long blonde hair. Despite the fact that I preferred slightly older children, I was a retired primary teacher, I could see that the little boy was by any standards very attractive too. He had a shock of blond hair, huge brown eyes and a beaming smile marred only by rather pointed teeth. As usual at the vets we talked about our animals. The little boy Jamie who was two years old tried to stroke my old cat, but she cowered back into her basket and began to mew plaintively. 'What's wrong with the puppy?' I asked, stroking it gently.

Melissa looked slightly embarrassed, 'They were playing together and he bit him.'

'Goodness,' I laughed, 'shouldn't you be at the doctors?'

'No, you don't understand, Jamie bit the puppy!'

At that moment I was called in to see the older vet, the only one who could cope with my cat's tantrums and when I came out Melissa and Jamie had gone.

Several weeks later I was in the local supermarket. I heard a call and turned round to see Jamie perched in a trolley waving to me. I bypassed the cake section and went to say hello. We chatted a bit about the problems of settling down in a new area and then I asked how the puppy was. Melissa looked distraught and then said, 'He had to be put to sleep, the bite got infected.'

I was very shocked. 'Poor Jamie,' I said, 'he must miss him.'

On hearing his name Jamie turned and smiled at me and again I was struck by how pointed his little white teeth were. We parted company and I invited Melissa to pop in any time she liked for a cup of tea.

Weeks passed and I saw nothing of them. I thought it a bit odd as she seemed such a pleasant girl and had appeared genuinely pleased with my invitation. After another month I decided to go round to see her. I couldn't believe my eyes, the house was closed up and there was a 'For Sale' board in the front garden. I stood there amazed wondering why the family had moved so quickly.

At that moment the front door of the house next door opened and a man came down the path. 'Excuse me,' I said, 'do you know where Melissa Harris has moved to?'

'Sad business, sad business,' he said, shaking his head, 'it was all so quick, at the doctor's one day, dead the next!'

'Dead!' I stood there paralysed with shock.' 'What happened?'

'Apparently she had a bad bite and it poisoned her whole system, all over in 48 hours.'

'And Jamie?' I said, 'what's happened to Jamie and his dad?'

'His dad died about a year ago just before they moved here, some mysterious illness, Melissa didn't like to talk about it.'

Seeing how upset I was the man laid a kindly hand upon my arm, 'If it's Jamie you're worried about, don't be, he's going to be alright. He's gone to live with his aunt and uncle. They're lovely people with three little children of their own and a house full of pets so things have worked out just fine for him!'

THE CARPENTER
R E Bilson

Doncaster ... midwinter!

Tom was making his way to work in his carpenter's van with his dog, Rupert, who went with him on every job. As he drove his van into the builder's yard, Bob, the foreman came out of his office shouting, 'Tom, I've got a job for you.'

Tom said, 'What job?'

'Putting floorboards in a cottage.'

'Where is this cottage?' said Tom.

'Near Skipton.'

'But how do I find the cottage?'

'Come in the office, Tom. I'll show you a map.'

Tom shouted out, 'That's in the wilds!'

'Do you think you can find it?'

Tom said nothing. He started loading his van up with floorboards. 'That's it,' he said to himself and loaded Rupert. 'Come on, we got a job to do.'

Tom's Story ...

As I was going along the road, I started to feel hungry. Then I saw a sign on the side of the road - '*Café ... a mile and a half*'.

As I pulled into the café yard, it started to snow.

'Rupert, you can stay in the van where it's warm. I'm going to buy myself a bacon roll and a mug of steaming hot coffee.'

I walked into the café. It had a friendly, warm feeling with five customers and myself. When I finished my meal, I said to the cook, 'I'd like the same meal for the dog, please.'

A lady sitting in the corner doing the crossword asked, 'What sort of dog is he?'

I said, 'Yorkshire terrier.'

I paid the bill then made my way outside into the cold. Rupert was waiting for me. 'Here you are, boy. Get that down yer.'

As I pulled away from the café, it was still snowing. When I had done six miles from the café, I saw a sign saying, '*Skipton*'. I said to myself, *where does this road turn off?*

As soon as I said that, there it was - a sign at the side of the snowy grass verge, 'To Highway Cottage'. It looks like nobody goes down this road. It looks like an old lane to me. Bushes and trees cover the right way.

About a hundred yards on, there it was, the cottage.

'Rupert, out you get and go look for rabbits.'

I started to unload the van. By then it had stopped snowing. Bob had said the key was in the letterbox on a piece of string. When I unlocked the door it opened like somebody stood behind me and gave it a big push. The room was cold, damp and dull looking with gas light fittings on the wall and an old-fashioned fireplace in the corner. I started pulling old floorboards up. With the wood, I made a fire.

I heard sounds like horses' hooves; like pulling a wagon. I went to the window then called Rupert. He came running and laid beside the fire. Then I heard footsteps and voices.

'That's funny! The dog doesn't bark; just lays there.'

I made my mind up to go outside to investigate. When I looked down, there were no wagon wheel markings nor footprints. I went back and looked round the side of the cottage at the side door. On there was a cross and some writing. I had a job to make it out. Then a voice said, 'Go now.' I'd heard that voice before; the voice of my father. He's been dead for eleven years!

I noticed it was getting dark all of a sudden so I went back into the cottage. 'Come on, Rupert. Let's get out of here.' The dog followed me to the van.

'Rupert, jump in. Stay there, boy.'

I forgot to get my tools so I had to go back. The room was in darkness; the fire had gone out so I had a job to find them - but at the end, I did.

As I made my way towards the van, music started to play like old-fashioned waltzes. This made me turn round. I had the fright of my life. The gaslights were on in the bedrooms and people were dancing. The music got louder and louder.

As I got in the van I said, 'Come on, Rupert. Let's go.'

*   *   *

Tom never did go back!

MYSTERIOUS MEETINGS
Annietta

1 January

Dear Daisy,

Happy New Year. I was sorry to hear you've been unwell, so I thought I'd write to cheer you up and tell you about me and Joe: a tale of Masonic mystery!

You know how fed up I've been with Joe's constant socialising? He's always off to Masonic meetings and organising this or that with his brothers. It makes me feel like he has no time to enjoy his own home. Well, I thought it's a new year, perhaps it's time to see what the attraction is in all this going out: my new year's resolution is to make an effort and take part more. Now I've made my mind up, I'm almost looking forward to meeting all the people he spends so much time with. I can't really imagine what's so wonderful about spending the evening with a lot of equally miserable men, although, you never know, it may stop the nagging. I might even find out why these meetings have to be so secretive.

I'll keep you up-to-date on my findings. I feel quite the detective looking at Joe's dark doings! Hopefully, it'll make us both feel better. Wish me luck!

Are you still in pain, dear? Keep it wrapped up, and take care.

Love Anne.

14 February

Dear Daisy,

Happy Valentine's Day. Did you get any romantic cards? I don't seem to, now we've been married a few years. Still, I did make an effort and told Joe I'd go to his Masonic Ladies Night dinner. I thought that might be romantic, and show him I'm trying.

It certainly took him by surprise, as he told me it was one date, then the next day told me it was another. I think it was the shock of my agreeing to go this year, it must have confused him no end: he was his usual attractive self, scowling for days afterwards! It does make you wonder what sort of dinner it can be, when he doesn't know what day it is!

Then he said he wants me to look really glamorous, and that I mustn't buy the dress by myself. Cheeky bugger, I hope he doesn't think he's coming with me. It would be a nightmare shopping with Mr High and Mighty. Do you know, his sisters said, when they were younger, he used to put his trousers under the mattress and make them all sit on the bed for an hour to press them - every day, though, not just for special occasions! And those shiny spats he wears look like a dandy cock's spurs. Would you believe it? If I'm not careful he'll probably dress me in a Masonic robe, just make sure it's right for the occasion! I had to laugh at the thought. Hope you do too.

Sorry to hear you've had a relapse. It's been festering so long now, you may be lucky and it'll drop off. If not, you could try wrapping a sweaty sock round it - they say the old remedies are the best!
Love Anne.

The Ides of March

Dear Daisy,

Hope you're feeling better, love. Sorry to hear you're still being troubled. You know I'd knock it off myself, if I could.

Well, what a to-do we've had here: Joe said he didn't want me to wear any of my old clothes, and that he wanted to buy me something to impress people. I could feel his extravagance getting the better of him, and his ambitions made his eyes burn red like the Devil's as the idea took hold. Where does he get them from? I must say, I'd rather have spent the money on some walking shoes and a winter coat, but Gentleman Joe had to have his way! His brother's wife, Joan, was brought round for the occasion, but we both nearly fainted when he put £50 on the table and said to her, as if I wasn't there, 'Take her shopping, will you, and don't let her buy anything sensible! She must look glamorous, more glamorous than anybody else's wife, or else!'

Or else what, I ask you? He should have married Mae West, not Anne Winterbottom: 5ft tall, 6 stone, and more used to working in a cotton mill than the silent films of his dreams! I do have naturally blonde hair, though ...

Well anyway, we found this powder blue chiffon dress, 'Matches your eyes, madam, and sequinned so elegantly', according to that 'I'm-too-good-for-this-job' shop assistant. It does look nice though, even if I do feel like something that fell off the Christmas tree. I decided to buy it when I noticed that gleam in Joan's eyes, you know: not quite jealousy but a long way from motherly love, as well. Never mind, I suppose we're both Masonic widows really. You have to wonder where he gets these ideas from? I'm not sure he's got an imagination, or if he has, it's a well kept secret! That's what happens when you marry in the middle of a war, you never really know them. Still, at least he survived being gassed in the trenches, for better or for worst.

I don't like the sound of your thingy going green! Have you been to the hospital with it?

I'll let you know about the do, not long to wait.
Love Anne.

1 April

Dear Daisy

Glad to hear you're feeling much better and it's not painful anymore.

I'm still recovering from the Ladies Evening and glad to be back in my winter woollies. You should have seen me floating about in chiffon, it would have cheered you up no end: the Femme Fatale of Wigan! I greeted every frozen smile and disapproving eyebrow with a Mae West 'Come up and see me some time' brazen smile. I'm not sure anyone appreciated the acting, and I had to button my lip, as old dagger eyes kept me by his side all night.

You'd have thought you were in a circus with the overdressed brittle brigade, and men behaving ever so strangely. They were banging on tables with hammers, and singing songs I'd never heard before. Joe seemed quite at home with it all. They were obviously getting in the mood for some building or demolishing of some kind, being Masons, I mean. Eh, but it did make me laugh when I thought about it. Maybe it's the after effects of the war? I suppose it could have turned their minds a bit, don't you?

That reminds me: I must find out what they get up to in those meetings. I heard whispers that they have some very strange rituals? Someone said they had to bare their breast at every meeting? How peculiar! It's all so secretive that they have to swear they won't tell anyone or talk about it to their wives.

Maybe you're right and I ought to have a closer look. Funny though, the other women seemed to think I was exaggerating the number of meetings Joe and his brothers went to. Perhaps they're more enthusiastic than most, what do you think?

Do take care. I know it's not green anymore, but it sounds huge. I think we'll have to try to meet up you know. Mother always said laughter's the best medicine!
Love Anne.

1st May

Well, Daisy,

I did it! All it took was a flat cap, a mac and nerves of steel. I kept my head down and followed them at a distance, just like Sherlock Holmes. Nobody really looked at me closely, although I was pushed about a bit in the overheated crowd they joined. I couldn't see much in the bustle, and was almost drowned in overcoats and deafened by the increasingly faster steps of those around me. The noise became louder and louder as we got nearer to two giant doors, and there was a definite air of expectation in the crowd. I know Masonic meetings are secretive, but you wouldn't believe how many anonymous men there were, faces hidden by their hats.

When I got through the doors, I was carried along in a crush of bodies until I grabbed a seat on the end of the row and held on for grim death. I thought I was going to be smothered with all those heavy breathers, sweaty brows and the smell of stale smoke - and, you know, it wasn't afternoon tea they'd been drinking before they got there!

Then a curtain was drawn back. What a revelation! It took my breath away! There was a lot more excitement in the air than any men only meeting could bring about (unless the local brothel had to share the miners' showers!) It wasn't the men baring their breasts and swearing allegiance to goodness knows what!

You should have seen her: all gaudy gown and flashing ankles! The hussy breathed in so deeply that when she sang her bosoms rose like the waves at Blackpool, heaving mountains of froth and promise! The men were rigid in their seats, all of them with at least their eyes popping out. And when she came to the edge of the stage, they were calling and clapping and some even swooning. What pillars of society! My mother always said that men's brains weren't in their heads!

Upright husbands? I've never seen such foolish men. They'd sell their souls to the devil for a kiss and a promise ... the strangest bunch of hooligans you ever did see. There he was with his brothers on the front row. If they'd got any closer they'd have ended up in prison! I've heard a Grand Master rules the Masons, but I don't know where he was that night!

When I think of the nagging I've endured after visiting my brother's pub, and yet those visits were like a convent outing in comparison to this 'Masonic meeting'. It'll be different from now on: we're going out together every time Joe and his brothers go to a 'meeting'.
Love Anne.

Daisy laughed out loud at her friend's description.

'I can't believe you really went to the music hall, and followed Joe in!'

'Well, here's to the first of many Guinness nights out we're going to have, Daisy. They say it puts iron in your blood, if not your soul, and at least it made that thing of yours drop off at last!'

'Good health!'

'Good health!'

THE SHADOW OF THE EAGLE
John London

The sun cast long shadows over Greenwich Park in the late summer afternoon as Tony and Jenny walked arm in arm through the park's rose garden. The garden was unusually deserted for the time of year.

'I say, Tony, we are entirely on our own, completely alone here!' exclaimed Jenny.

'Maybe it's meant to be. Just you and me, darling,' laughed Tony. 'Adam and Eve in our own Eden.'

As we walked on we gradually became aware that the atmosphere was slowly changing. What had up to then been a gentle breeze was becoming stiffer and stiffer until, all at once, as they turned the corner to the duck pond they were met by a sudden great gust of wind, which almost swept them into the water. The ducks were scattering about in panic, quacking furiously. And then, all was still. There was a strange feeling in the air. Jenny clung to Tony.

'It's scary, love!' she said. 'What is it? I've never felt like this before.'

'Me, neither,' came his reply.

Just then, their attention was attracted to a lone rose bush to the right of where they were standing, by the bank of the pond. Although all was now hushed and static, the bush was swaying violently as if the wind was still blowing. A strange whirring sound was also emanating from it. The roses it contained were changing colour, amazingly, as they watched. From deep red to purple to gold and back to red. Then a light, gradually getting brighter and brighter surrounded the bush until it shone with such an iridescence that they had to shield their eyes. All at once, they were aware of a presence. Was it human? A ghost perhaps? As they looked on the light dimmed, the bush stopped swaying and the roses returned to their original colours. Above the bush a great golden eagle hovered. It spoke.

'Have no fear, my children,' it said in a low, penetrating tone, 'for you are greatly blessed. To you the secrets of the park have been revealed.'

'Why us? And who are you?' asked Tony, greatly astonished.

'I am life itself. I do the walk of life for all living things. And you are the chosen ones, guaranteed to know the secrets of the great park. To you it has been given, and even more, if you care to know.'

'But what do we have to know, and why?' asked Jenny. 'And what is it that makes us so special?'

'Do not ask. If you want to know these things you must not question why. What is to be, is.'

The young couple were now greatly intrigued, although being in no fear of this apparition, but both were greatly puzzled and mystified by the bizarre situation they had inadvertently found themselves in. 'We would be fascinated by whatever you have to tell us,' said Tony.

'You are not here to be fascinated. You are here to learn,' said the great eagle. 'When I was formed, at the dawn of creation, I was granted infinitely far-sighted vision. I can see right across the Earth, across the universe and far into the future as well as the distant past. Your names are written down before the mists of time arose.'

'Gosh!' said Tony, 'I must be pretty ancient!'

'Do not joke!' said the eagle as it hovered, motionless. 'But look! You both have something that you must do. Each of you, come, pluck a rose from my bush.'

As they did so they both slightly pricked their fingers on the stems of each rose.

'You see, as Shakespeare wrote in his play As You Like It, 'He who would sweetest rose find will find love's prick'. So it goes, in any labour of love you have to take the rough along with the smooth,' said the eagle, with a knowing twinkle in his eye. 'So knowing the secrets of the park carries a similar responsibility.'

'Tell us please, the secrets, then,' said Tony.

'You will learn them by what you do,' said the eagle. 'This then, is what you both must do.'

As he said this he rose up and flew round the pond seven times.

'Now you two must walk around the pond seven times.'

'Strange request, but I suppose we must comply. After all, stranger things happened in Tales From The Arabian Nights,' said Jenny.

As they started their journey they were both aware that not a sound could be heard anywhere. All was silent, no birds could be heard singing. Not even the sound of a rustle of a branch or of leaves could be heard. Not even their own footfalls could be heard. Tony turned to his partner to make mention of this. He opened his mouth but no sound came out. He couldn't speak! Neither could Jenny. When at last they had circumnavigated the body of water for the seventh time, suddenly all was alive with sound again! They marvelled at the variety and diversity of sounds that nature yielded and their hearts swelled with appreciation for both that and for regaining the ability to hear and communicate with each other. Hearing a chuckling sound they turned and there above the rose bush was their old friend the eagle, who said, 'Do you now appreciate the secret of the gift of hearing?'

They both nodded in agreement.

'And now, my beloved, you must perform a second task.' As he said this he flew to the other end of the pond and back.

'Now both of you pick up the roses that you plucked (They had left them on one of the seats facing the pond) and carry them to the far side of the pond and cast them into the waters.'

At the instant that they started toward the far side of the pond they were suddenly engulfed by a great darkness.

'What do we do now?' asked Jenny, 'it seems to be another test, but we have our ears to guide us.

'Listen!' replied Tony.

And they could hear the leaves of the trees rustling to the right of them and the waters lapping the bank to their left. So very slowly they kept to a route in the middle of the two. Gradually they gained the far bank and as they did the darkness immediately lifted and bright sunlight lit the whole aspect. As they cast their roses into the water they marvelled at the varied colours of the birds and flowers and the whole beauty of creation.

Making their way back they could hear their friend, this time cackling like a gigantic rook.

'Do you now appreciate the secret of the gift of seeing?'

They both nodded again, marvelling.

'Now for your third task. Go and both eat fifty blackberries each from that bramble over there. The berries wear black, ripe and juicy.

'At last, a task we can thoroughly enjoy!' said Tony.

As he bit heartily into the first few that he plucked he exclaimed, 'They have no taste whatsoever!'

Jenny was similarly disappointed. They looked at their friend who quietly repeated, 'Fifty.'

One hundred tasteless blackberries between them later and Tony said, 'OK job done.'

And they both turned and faced the eagle.

'Now, my friends, eat seven more,' he said.

Reluctantly they picked seven each and, tasting them, found them to be exquisitely delightful to the palate.

'I've never tasted anything so delicious in my life!' exclaimed Tony.

'Similarly my friends, with the secret of the gift of taste,' said the eagle with a smile.

At this instant Jenny suddenly dropped to the ground.

'Jenny! Darling! What's the matter?' sobbed Tony as he cradled her in her arms. He felt her pulse. There was none. 'Oh no! What have you done?' he screamed at the eagle.

'Don't ask me. I can't stop people dying,' he replied.

'Oh, my Jenny, it can't be! Don't leave me now!' and he wept uncontrollably.

'Maybe it isn't. Maybe she hasn't,' said the eagle, consolingly. 'Tony my friend, take another rose from my bush and lay it on her heart.' As he laid the rose over Jenny's heart, she at once opened her eyes.

'Tony, dear, where have I been? I was having this lovely dream about a magic eagle.'

'But he's here,' said Tony looking round at the rose bush.

But both the eagle and the bush had gone, had vanished without trace.

As they were leaving the park arm in arm, Tony thought he could hear a voice echoing from the rose garden saying, 'So now you know also the secret of the preciousness of the gift of love, which is not only the secret of the park, but of *the whole world!*'

THE BALLAD OF THE OUTLAWS' CLEARING
Carly Dugmore

With his thick black hair falling o'er his neck, gleaming blue-black, like jays in the sun, he cleaned out the spurs on his best riding boots, spat and polished the barrel of his gun. At the outlaws' clearing he stood out from the crowd, grief etched deep down to the pores on his face. Determination bid him live, held him up like a staff; misery draped over him like death's black cape.

He'd been a boy, twelve years past, that dreadful night on the road, wanted only pocket-watch and coins from the noble man. But thunder devilled the horse: the pistol clipped his hilt; the corpse lay before him, white eyes at half slant. The rain lashing down, he rout to find flame; rooks circled like smoke demons 'bove the pyre. Lightning screamed through the sky like a forked mandrake root; he took to the heather - set it afire.

Cold cloaked years passed, then like a bright shooting star, she ripped through his mind 'til he begged it be still. In a twinkling, bewitched was his hardness of heart; the voice of his saviour, she said, 'I am Lil.' '

'Twas love from the start, the sheriff's daughter and he, swathed in liberty, sweetness, mischief. Fluted laughter escaped her as he twirled her in dance, touched his lips to the young maiden's cheek.

'Neath the bonny rose moon of summer's sweet dusk, on nest o' heather and moss from the moor, he traced the mark at her breast with the feather from his hat; used his pistol to latch shut the barn door ...

Lo, the baby arrived with the cord round his neck, in the cold haunted stillness of night. No herbs could save her - her blood would not clot; Lil died without knowledge or fight.

The sheriff's men had then driven the outlaw from town; desolation crushed his heart like the kick of a horse. They forbade him take one look at his newborn son; his cries had echoed on the winds of the moors. So, under blanket of night, cloaked by canvas of cloud, his horse now galloped off with a burst. Dark eyes ablaze from the maelstrom within: love was his hunger, revenge his thirst.

Above the small county gaol, the sheriff's wife rocked the crib, quenched the candle, bid welcome the night. She did not see the outlaw steal away with the boy clutched to his chest like a vial of anodyne. At the outlaws' clearing they swapped travellers' tales, the fire's flames licking warmth to their cheeks. They played brag for black dogs 'til the dram still ran dry; spitted wild boar for a celebratory feast.

The babe was anointed under Diane's shadow'd guard, the baptismal sword scything a cross above his forehead. But the vesture of reverence was angel visit to be: rancorous reality soon occulted their fête. At ten of the clock, horses' hooves could be heard; in the distance, two shots of a gun. *Bang! Bang!* The cavalry surrounded the camp in a flash; five bandits dead before any could run.

The battle ensued, but nightblind were the men, their knives cutting bluntly into the pitch. They were laid out to bear north, facing Satan's unholy door, oozing the red, viscid resin of Hade's crypt. At last, the sheriff stared him down like the shadow of Death, omen's raven cawed the funeral bell. 'Bell, book and candle cannot save you now; You're black buried: gone to all hell!'

Though it entered from behind, he still witnessed the death; jewels of blood wept a crucifix on his gown. He fell to the earth with the chilling last cry: 'Oh, dear God no - who'll raise my son now?'

The last embers of fire snuffed out by the dirt, the wind still and silent, as it from affright, his eulogy was delivered by the solemn hoot of an owl; a lone bloodied bloom marked the spot where he died.

She swayed in the mist, like a young faerie queen, eyes like cut sapphire, hair rippling like a stream. A smile kissed her lips as she knelt to the bairn, 'We'll raise him together, a family again.'

At the outlaws' clearing, during confetti of spring, one by one, the translucent figures did loom. Held court midst a turret of twisted oak trees; their laughter hanging on t' horn of a waxing moon.

Seventeen years passed, the outlaw's boy was now man, robed in riding coat of rich blackberry velvet. He rubbed sandalwood oil o'er the bristles of his jaw, spat and polished his sword-bayonet. He waited 'til the stars cast the night's only luminaire, cantered by escort of nightingales trill. His lilac eyes shimmered like the celestial land above; he descended the winding staircase of the hills.

He stole through her window - a true minion of the moon: she slept, framed by curls the colour of blushed shame. He laid a clutch of wild violets at the crest of her throat, brushed her lips with a kiss of lambent flame. At break of sun's blood, he knelt, plight his troth, the sheriff's daughter his trove of treasure and trance. But like his father before him his courtship was doomed, filched by fortune's voluptuous hand.

'Son, she'll be thine when the Devil is blind, for the mortal-bound cannot soar with spiritual ghost.'

As lightning through oak, the revelation split his core: the same bullet had killed son and father both! He clung to his father as seventeen years afore, sank to the earth, a tortured gargoyle of pain. He clawed the dust of his grave with his icy fingertips. He died all over again.

So, on a bright, cloudless night, eternity swallowing the moors, the moss-grown graves 'scribed with roscid leaves, he whispers his love, though she'll never hear, never has, 'My sweet, with the violets I'll return to thee.'

And the sheriff's young daughter restlessly wanders the heath, drawn by a presence she does not understand. Lifts her tear-stained cheek to be dried by the wind; feels the gentle phantom stranger take her hand.

IT'S DARK OUT THERE
Caroline Lake

Molly froze, waking with sweat trickling down her forehead and tears swelling in her eyes.

'Help!' she choked as she envisioned the knife still up to her neck. Her eyes were wide like a risen corpse and the image of the stranger's face was fixed in her head. She clutched her throat still feeling the splitting sensation. Her breathing mellowed as she realised her body was intact.

Looking at her clock it was 12am and outside darkness still surrounded her. *No,* she thought, *please not this. Let it not be real.*

Turning the bedside lamp on, her room became dimly lit with a pink shade. Her brown hair was ruffled, her curls wild, as she sat at the edge of the bed. The phone rang. *What the devil? Who is that?* she thought, picking up the receiver.

'Molly?' A muffled voice screamed. 'It's me … Sam.' Her voice was piercing ...

Probably drunk again Molly thought. *Why can't she sort her life out. Go to bed early, get a good job and act like a normal person.*

'Molly,' Sam squealed, 'are you there?'

'Yes, what's up?' Rubbing her head, Molly tried to hear through the crackles.

'He won't stop following me. I know he's around here somewhere.'

'Who?' asked Molly, now wide awake. 'Where are you?'

Sam had been a wreck and getting into trouble since she separated from her husband, constantly on an alcoholic binge.

'In Park Lane. I left the pub and there's someone following me, he disappears then appears smoking a fag.'

'You're five minutes from home aren't you?' Molly figured out.

'No … I turned a different way. Molly I'm lost!'

Sam had not long moved to this area. Molly felt like her mother, feeling her pain at the loss of the marriage.

'Call the police! I'm on my way.' Molly answered.

'But what do I do? Oh God help me he's here again.'

'Sam call the cops on your mobile and go to the nearest house. I'm on my way.'

Slamming the phone down, Molly grabbed her shoes and coat, then her car keys. She didn't care about going out in her long, granny-looking nightie tonight. She knew this person was stalking, she could feel it in her bones.

Heading down the stairs, she nearly tripped over the cat's play mouse. Stabilising herself on the railings she continued round the hallway corner and to the front door. Molly knew time was everything, poor Sam would be in a right state. Opening the front door, she dashed out and locked it behind her, then unlocked her car and slipped in, slamming the blue door.

She turned the ignition key, it revved with persistence. Putting on her belt she looked out of the window and swung the car out of the driveway. The screeching of the tyres, she thought would wake the street as she sped off like a mad woman.

Molly had heard of Park Street. She was sure it was by a park and at this time of night it would be virtually deserted.

Turning the corner, her headlights flickered as she went over a hump in the road. 'Don't go on me now,' she pleaded, 'that would be all I need. What on Earth is Sam doing out again at this time of night alone? Has she no brains? Why do some people think it will never happen to them? Molly hoped she was wrong about Sam being in need, she wished that Sam had listened to her. She was pretty, intelligent with dark mahogany-coloured hair, but she was a mess in her head, her life turned upside down by her husband's adultery.

Turning another corner, Molly put some pressure on the brake then hit the accelerator as she straightened up the vehicle. 'I'm sure it's just around the next exit,' she pondered, checking the next street sign, 'yes, that's it!'

Turning the steering wheel, she ventured into the park's car park to see flashing lights illuminating the area like an invasion of UFOs.

The back of the ambulance was open and two men got out, dressed in pastel green. Pulling up the car beside the alarmed vehicle, Molly darted out as two police cars swung in behind her.

'We need you to stay back Miss,' the ambulance man ordered.

'Have you got her?' a cop asked the paramedic.

'We can't see her anywhere,' he replied.

Molly's throat felt tight as a shiver ran through her spine as though her body had been invaded. In her mind she saw the shadow of a dark man. 'A killer,' she whispered under her breath.

'Pardon?' the police officer said as the others started to scout the area and move bushes' leaves. 'Mrs Brown … Sam Brown?' they called out.

'What's going on? What's happened?' Molly raced, shaking.

'I'd like to ask you the same question,' the policeman said, his eyes glaring.

'Sam rang me saying she was being followed by someone. I got the impression it was a man. She said he was smoking. I told her to ring the police,' Molly rattled, staring.

The park was only small and she couldn't see Sam anywhere. She wondered whether she had passed her on the way, but Molly knew she hadn't.

'You'd better stay with us, we may want you to answer some questions,' he added.

'You haven't answered mine yet,' she snapped, 'she's a friend. Why an ambulance?'

'There was a call from a Mrs Brown from a mobile, screaming. She said she was running and someone was chasing her, then the connection was lost.

'Over here,' an officer called.

All the officers quickly moved over to a hedgerow. Molly couldn't go, she leaned against the nearest tree. *Please let her be okay* she thought.

Pain struck at the throat, she felt her body feeling blows of force as his face appeared. '*No!*' she screamed.

The tallest cop ran towards her as Molly clutched her neck. The officer grabbed her and she came out of her trance. ' A killer!' she choked. 'Death!'

'We've found her. God what a mess!' the ambulance man yelled.

The officer grabbed Molly once more. 'I think you'd better come with me,' he suggested.

Her eyes were wide with fear as she saw the killer in him.

'Don't touch me!' she screamed, standing and viewing the paramedics zipping up a body bag. 'No!' she sobbed.

Being pushed into a police car with cuffs placed on her wrists, Molly sobbed as the cop shut the door and started the engine. 'I'm innocent, what are you doing? What's happened?'

'It seems your beloved friend is dead,' he replied boldly, 'and you at this moment in time were around the scene and knew where she was. That in my eyes makes you a suspect. Someone has done this and someone is going down. You were clutching your throat, why?'

'I receive visions, dreams,' Molly rattled.

'Codswallop!' he bit, racing forwards and viewing her in the mirror.

'I do,' Molly wept. 'I didn't kill her.'

He turned round sharply, viewing her face as if he was looking to see if she really was psychic. 'You didn't kill her, but you knew she was dead before I told you. Slit across the throat.'

Molly clutched her head and started to rock, 'I didn't do it,' she bellowed.

He turned, facing the front again and smiled. 'You made it easy,' he answered.

'What?' she queried.

'To be caught?'

'But?' she stuttered.

He interrupted her. 'But ...' he sarcastically copied, 'I didn't do it. Well guess what lady ... I don't care!'

Molly stopped sobbing, her body froze in fear as his dark eyes watched her from the rear view mirror. 'I don't like you and you are an easy target.'

'What are you on about? You're sick! Let me out of here ... now!'

'Let you go? Of course I can't. The only place you'll be going is to jail or six-foot under.' Turning the key, the ignition started and he reversed.

'I mean it, you're mad!' she yelled.

Swinging out of the car par he looked back. 'You goody-two-shoes psychics think you can save the world but you forget you little white sheep half the time can't even save yourselves, and the wolf always gets his sheep.'

Molly tried opening the door, but it was locked.

'You can't run, you can't hide. Do you know why?'

She shook her head, her mouth tightly shut as he pulled over.

'Because I'm with law,' he grinned.

A man entered the front passenger seat. He was well built and wearing all black. 'That will teach her for wanting to go back to her husband,' he told the officer.

The cop shook his head. 'Last time I protect you,' he growled, 'but guess what?'

The stranger turned. Molly's heart stopped for a few seconds as their faces were virtually identical. *The killer,* she thought, *there's two?*

'That's right,' the cop's voice echoed in her head, 'and I'm going to kill you.'

Molly could see he meant it. He was the one she saw in the dream, the one that might murder her. 'Never!' she screamed, lunging forward, grabbing the steering wheel. The car swung round, crashing into a tree. The bumper crinkled like paper, their bodies went limp.

The following police car swung up beside them and the policeman grabbed his radio. As he opened the door and saw the strange man with a knife and Molly, he called the other officer over. 'Get the ambulance here right now!' he rattled, then took the knife.

Asleep, Molly dreamed of freedom and peace. She saw Sam walking into the light like an angel ascending into Heaven.

'Forgive me,' Molly pleaded, 'I failed you.'

'No,' Sam whispered like a breeze, 'I'm free and you were meant to help me.' Sam took another step as if she was walking up an invisible ladder. 'I'll be watching you,' Sam said with a smile that warmed, 'and I'll never forget you.'

A tear trickled down Molly's face as she woke to a new start and the bleeping sound of the heart monitor, three months later.

An Elizabethan Murder
Ellen Spriring

The court of Elizabeth was rife with rumour. Lord Robert Dudley had returned to court and immediately had been thrown into the tower. Treason was the crime. Branded as a traitor for betrayal of the queen's majesty.

Lord Robert had dalliances with several ladies of the court, he was a 'blue-blooded' male and such men do not live by bread alone. The queen was a jealous woman, particularly, where 'her eyes', Lord Robert was concerned. Elizabeth was astute and something did not ring true.

As chief 'lady of the bed chamber' I was privy to most things. I saw and heard much, was told secrets but said naught. That way I stayed 'confidant' to the queen and kept my head safely on my shoulders.

It had all started with the mysterious death of Sir John Appleby, a knight of the realm with connections to Lord Robert. He had been poisoned by an unknown hand. There was always intrigue at court and a jostling for power and the royal ear and favour. It was said that the Lady Mary Appleby had somewhat of a 'roving eye' and had cast more than a casual glance in Lord Robert's direction.

As a favourite of the queen in fact 'the favourite', he ought to have known better than to encourage the lady, especially as she was a married lady too.

Elizabeth missed nothing and the news soon reached the royal ear, she was beside herself with anger. 'God's death, what is Lord Robert about this time? Will he play fast and loose with the ladies of my court, yet still implicate himself in a murder of a knight of my realm and sully my reputation into the bargain? I think not indeed! Get him hence to the tower!'

It was duly carried out.

'Kat Ashley, where are you?' my mistress called.

I did as I was bid. Her pride was hurt as was her ego. I had seen her thus so many times, her fragile nerves were in tatters. 'How dare he, Robin, dear Robin.' She loved him but at this moment in time, she would make him pay. If he was guilty her ministers would expect it. He would go to 'the block', Lord Robert will lose his head for his folly. Elizabeth was adamant. She ranted and raved, sobbed her heart out upon my shoulder, there was much comfort to give. I despaired for her, for night after night she paced her rooms with no sleep to speak of, I feared for her sanity.

The Lady Appleby was in disgrace, banned from court and under house arrest until the unsavoury business was over and the culprit or culprits were found. The queen's spies were everywhere. Lord Robert had been unpopular, was too powerful and had the ear of the queen. He had many enemies, it would suit the queen's council to find Lord Robert implicated in the murder.

Queen Elizabeth had many enemies at home and abroad, the Catholic faction, and although she had a liberal view and allowed her subjects to worship as they would, she would not tolerate scandal near her person. She ordered an investigation and appeared determined to get answers. Meanwhile Lord Robert had to 'cool his heels' in the tower. As for myself, Kat Ashley, I kept my own council, being careful to keep her majesty calm and taking her side, when asked for my humble opinion as as her 'dear friend'.

In previous months there had been numerous visits to the Appleby estates by Lord Robert. The reason given for this was to improve the management of the estate. All of the servants were questioned. One of them had been tortured by the queen's own minister on 'the rack' in order to get him to implicate Lord Robert in the murder, but the manservant held true and no information was extracted from him. Nothing could be proved, the manservant left his place of torture a broken man, in more ways than one.

At this time numerous poisons could be obtained if the person procuring the substance could pay well. This usually meant that they would be of high rank in the court and the deed would be well planned, well hidden and well paid. So who?

Elizabeth turned her attention to Lady Appleby, who was brought to the tower for further questioning. Lord Robert was released for the moment, but banned from court. My mistress would never allow the erring pair to he under the same roof, tongues could wag and the situation made much of, or so the queen implied. I knew that the woman Elizabeth was very jealous and did not trust Robert's friends. A liaison could be arranged had she not herself been imprisoned in the tower years ago and meetings arranged for her and Lord Robert during that time. Oh no the queen did not trust him.

It emerged that Lord Appleby was done to death while his wife was visiting the queen's dear cousin Bess of Hardwick. She had travelled to Hardwick Hall by carriage, the weather had taken a turn for the worst and she had stayed overnight. that meant that Lady Appleby had an alibi.

Elizabeth was not satisfied. There had to be a third party, someone in the pay of Lady Appleby. The queen was furious of that possibility. 'Hell's teeth does he and she think I was born yesterday. Her aim was to rid herself of a husband and have Lord Robert to boot.' The queen ranted and raved. 'A God's curse on Dudley.' In public.

In private Elizabeth was broken-hearted at the prospect of her 'beloved eye's' betrayal.

Lady Appleby's maidservants were questioned, her lady of the bedchamber was tortured. Under that torture confessed to putting poison in her master's wine, because of is connection with Lord Robert and that she had been well paid by her mistress, who has also been well paid by another. No person was named. What she was not privy to could not implicate the anonymous 'villain of the piece'. So endeth the life of one of Elizabeth's peers.

What of reprisals? This story had also cast suspicion on the queen's complicity in the deed. I had never seen her so angry and beside herself with rage. 'God's death I smell treason. Nay I can taste it! Heads will roll, I vow it.'

Heads did indeed roll. Lady Appleby's servant went to 'the block' as did the unfortunate Lady Appleby. Yet what of the third person. It was conceded that it was a political enemy of both the queen and Lord Robert , as her ministers and council were in favour of that explanation. Thus taking the blame from them and the queen's majesty, if they had to give the benefit of the doubt for the queen's favourite, well so be it, that as the easiest way of placating Elizabeth.

The years rolled by and in due course Lord Robert was given an earldom. He was now the Earl of Leicester, this was engineered by the queen, who had been too patient for too long in humouring her ministers on the question of her marriage.

They were afraid she would succumb to Robert's wishes and marry him. This was in fact, what she wanted to do, he was her love, her life, her 'eyes' her dear Robin.

When he was given his 'rewards' she showed him obvious affection by stroking his beard and tickling him under his chin, to say nothing of what she did in the privacy of her rooms. Only I, Kat Ashley was privy to that. She was so happy, she was in love.

After a while Lord Robert became impatient and married a lady of the court without Elizabeth's permission. A big mistake. When the royal ear was told of this, she became like a mad woman. She paced her rooms, wringing her hands as was her habit when stressed, she stamped her feet and showed her temper like a child, flinging herself down on her bed, sobbing and screaming insults. Woe betide anyone who came near her in that demise. I found myself in the role of comforter, confidant, friend, punch-bag and being ten years Elizabeth's senior, quite often a mother figure, the mother Elizabeth never had. Anne Boleyn had been executed in her daughter's infancy.

Elizabeth eventually forgave him, although she did not forget. She declared herself 'married to England', 'a virgin queen' for all to see. The 'Gloriana' that was expected of a monarch such as herself. She did reign until 1603 and it was a wonderful queenship. It did not please her ministers that she did not marry, but she maintained an air of majesty in her dealings with them and was Robert's guardian angel during his last years. The queen lovingly nursed him when he became ill and when he died, shut herself away in such sorrow, locking his last letter away and with it, her heart.

I suffered with her and for her. She was not only my queen but my child in some ways. I was, above all, her loving subject who would see no harm come to her and would and did what I could to protect her vulnerability. My actions had made me break her laws, I felt that she had known of my actions and complicity in the deed done to save her from herself. A deed of murder that had gone wrong.

The twist was that Lady Appleby's maidservant had given the poison to her master, not her mistress as it should have been. All that had come out under pain of torture was true to them, but not to 'the third person', one Kat Ashley who had been protector of the queen's majesty. The 'villain of the piece'.

WANTED FOR MURDER
Nolan Maxie

It was a late Sunday night in mid-September, about 11.30 and my partner, Texas Highway Patrolman John Odom, said that he wasn't feeling well and asked me to drop him off at his house. He would go off duty for the day a little early. We had been working since one that afternoon and we were due to terminate our shift at midnight. Believe me, I was ready to go home too. But, just a few minutes after I dropped him off and as I was preparing to close out my day, there came a broadcast on my state police radio. The broadcast was coming from our Texas DPS District Headquarters' base radio station in Tyler, Texas. The radio broadcast said ...

'Attention all officers, all stations, *wanted for murder* by the Houston Police Department, occurring on Scott Street at approximately 6.45pm this date, Elviron Monroe Lewis Jr, 5'10", weighing 185lbs and driving a blue and white 1958 Chevrolet 4 door sedan. Subject may be headed to relatives at either of 2 locations, Lubbock, Texas or Paris, Texas. *Consider armed and dangerous - Approach with caution.'* (end broadcast)

The broadcast also gave the licence plate number of the suspect's automobile and said that a small child, aged 5 or 6, might be riding with him. I quickly figured ... it's about a 4½ to 5 hour drive from here to Houston and if this suspect is going to Paris tonight, then he will be travelling north on Highway 19 right here through Sulphur Springs. So, he should be getting close to me right about now. I thought, *maybe I can get this one tonight.* It has been a really quiet shift thus far.

As I was now patrolling alone late at night (which wasn't really a rare occurrence but sometimes a little scary), I now had to move quickly if I was going to have a good chance of intercepting this murder suspect, right here, tonight. So I proceeded quickly out Highway 19, heading south from town, crossing over 1-30. As I patrolled along, I was looking at every licence plate number that I met. My headlights reflected on each front licence plate.

After travelling about a mile down Highway 19, the 4th car I met, a blue and white 1958 Chevrolet, reflected the licence plate number that I was looking for. Eureka! That was it! The apprehension of a possibly armed felony suspect is imminent. The heart pumps faster. The adrenaline starts to flow. *Consider armed and dangerous!* I began to get seriously prepared.

I quickly swung my patrol car out onto the right shoulder and made a U-turn. Pulling up behind the suspect vehicle I again confirmed the vehicle description and the licence plate number: a hit for sure. I would like to get a back-up police unit in the vicinity real soon.

Highway 19, at that time, turned into West Main Street into downtown Sulphur Springs. I slowly trailed the suspect until we entered the Sulphur Springs city limits. All the time, I was advising Tyler DPS radio and the Sulphur Springs Police Department radio, that the broadcast that was put out just a few minutes ago, I now had that suspect under surveillance. I requested the SPPD to provide me with a back-up police unit on W Main Street.

Now, I was only a short distance west of the Courthouse Square. Just past the SSPD building and the city water tower, I met their police car. At that time I turned on my flashing red lights and began pulling the suspect car over. He stopped and just in case he still had with him the high powered rifle used in the murder, before getting out of my patrol car, I secured my own heavy firepower. 'Approach with caution!' Along with the SSPD, we requested that the suspect exit his vehicle and put his hands on top of the car. He wisely offered no resistance.

As had been reported, the young child was in the car. There were no weapons in the car and he advised us that he was headed to Paris, Texas. Upon searching his pockets, one 30-30 calibre carbine cartridge was found on him. They said he had gone to his place of employment, broken into his boss' office and taken the 30-30 rifle. They said he went and committed murder and took custody of *his* child. He then returned the rifle to his boss' office and left town. It seemed to be a typical domestic triangle. He said that this child was the only one that belonged to him.

The suspect was jailed at Sulphur Springs PD until Houston officers arrived to take him back to Houston for formal charges. The child was placed with the local Children's Protection Service to be turned over to relatives later.

The next day was Monday, my regular day off. I went fishing on Lake Tawakoni down in Rains County. When I later told my partner what had happened after I let him out at home, he just replied, 'I was really sleeping soundly and am glad you made it OK without me.'

Two or three months later, I was required to travel to Houston to the Harris County Courthouse for the defendant's court proceedings on murder charges. The judge sentenced him to 25 years in the Texas prison system.

While back in Houston, I visited some old friends and former work associates that I hadn't seen in a great long while. It didn't take very long though, with all the excitement around Houston and the 'never a dull moment' activity at the Houston Regional DPS Headquarters, for me to know that I needed to return to North Texas real soon. And I did.

This case was an easy one.

UNFINISHED BUSINESS
Stephen Humphries

If it hadn't been such a slow afternoon I never would have noticed the advert in the newspaper. An exhibition of tropical fish run by a group of enthusiasts, with a competition for best in show and a cash prize for the winner. I took a passing interest in fish since I was a kid, but had never progressed beyond amateur status, ignorance and forgetfulness usually resulting in my fish doing the backstroke within a few months of taking up residence. I was looking for an excuse to leave work early and thought I could leave now with a clear conscience in an attempt to beat the rush hour traffic.

The address was vaguely familiar, but was a long detour from my normal route home. If memory served me right this neighbourhood was mentioned more often in the crime pages of the local newspaper than the ideal homes section of its supplement. It was rumoured that even the dogs went around in twos out there!

After a couple of wrong turns I finally found the area and drove into a large council estate. Row upon row of identical houses slid past, neglect and defeat hanging heavy in the air. After a couple of circuits I came upon what was charmingly referred to as the community centre, though it wouldn't have looked out of place in any of the urban hot spots around the world. The usual graffiti announced the pecking order of the local youth and two large doors stood open in greeting, below the place where the security camera once held sway, before it was stolen. I almost expected to see defensive firing positions in the heavily barred windows though could make none out with my untrained eye. I searched for a parking space in the nearby streets, wondering if I'd made the right decision coming here at all, and regretting the fact that I was driving my own car. A space was available outside the local Asian take-away, whose owner saw more action now than when he taught unarmed combat to the local police force back in his native land. I parked behind an old Ford that I thought had customised suspension, 'til I noticed the reason for its extra height was the four cinder blocks where the wheels used to be. Double checking that I'd locked the car, I started to walk towards the community centre when I was hailed from behind.

'Hey mister, can we mind your car?'

Two ten-year-old boys stood there, expertly weighing me up. They looked the same and dressed the same and for a moment I thought the circus might be in town. I walked back with a patronising smile upon my face.

'Don't touch that car, son, I have a big dog in the back,' I lied casually.

'He can put out fires, can he?' asked the second of this sinister double act.

Streetwise beyond their years, they seemed to weigh me up and I imagined I could see the words 'pigeon' and 'easy' glide across their faces, which is strange because I couldn't read minds before today. I tried to meet their cynical smirks but failed miserably. I emptied all my loose change into an outstretched grubby little hand and made a mental note to check my insurance policy. From the look of disdain on their faces I wished I did have a big dog in the back and wondered if I was soon to be the proud owner of four new cinder blocks.

At the entrance to the hall another outstretched hand greeted me, this one requesting an entry fee. I dually obliged, suspecting that he might be a blood relative of the gruesome twosome who were shaking down innocent motorists around the corner, they had the same deadpan eyes. Inside, small groups of people stood around talking and laughing and I began to relax a bit. The fish were exhibited in small glass tanks, each fish having its own individual tank. Hiding my unease, I went through the motions of looking at each exhibit. Some of the owners stood nearby, daring anyone to criticise. I could identify most of the species, but was too intimidated to ask the names of the ones I didn't know. Feeling out of place, I made my way along the entries, counting about twenty exhibits in total. I practised what I hoped was my thoughtful look and knowing nod at each fish, who each in turn ignored me completely. Conversations died as I approached and resumed as I passed, owners taking stock of this outsider. I got the feeling I wasn't measuring up, or that could have been just my persecution complex kicking in.

'Excuse me,' a voice called from one of the groups, 'you couldn't help us out, could you?'

Fearing I was being asked to put my hand in my pocket yet again, I turned to meet the smiling face of a middle-aged man and yet another outstretched hand, this time in greeting. I took it gratefully, noticing my own sweaty palm.

'You wouldn't happen to be an expert on these sorts of things, would you? It's just that our judge hasn't shown up and as an impartial outsider you might be able to pick a winner for us? What do you say; will you have a stab at it?'

'No judge, huh?' I echoed, trying to think on my feet, and failing. Maybe it was more than just winners they took a stab at?

'Yes, well I'm afraid they're a bit of a competitive lot here and there was some unpleasantness at the last show when the places were awarded.'

'Unpleasantness?' I repeated uneasily.

'Well, let's just say more than a few feelings were bruised.'

'Oh, well, hmm, no, sorry, but I'm really hopeless at things like this.'

'Oh come on, what's the worst that can happen?'

My schoolboy imagination went into overdrive. What indeed?

'Oh but I couldn't, I'm not really qualified enough to make a judgement. I wouldn't know an angel from a cichlid I'm afraid.'

'An angel is a cichlid,' replied my tormentor, and he couldn't keep the disdain from his voice.

'Well, there you go, you see, I'd be hopeless,' I said, and my laughter sounded hollow even to my ears.

'Well, if he doesn't show up soon we may call on you,' he said, moving away, and gave me the impression it wouldn't be a social call.

Now worried as well as uneasy, I continued my inspection of exhibits, refusing to make eye contact with any of the belligerent owners.

My reputation and possibly my hide were saved by the arrival of the judge. A small man with mean eyes, he strode to the table in the centre of the room, clutching a motorcycle helmet beneath his arm as if his life depended on it, and maybe it did. His anorak hung loosely from his bony shoulders, revealing an array of coloured pens in his breast pocket. His bulging Filofax hinted that maybe he might have already made up his mind. I was glad to see the hostile stares switched to him, along with a couple of angry hisses, though I admit that could have been the doors. I stood back to watch the show.

With a smile that wouldn't have looked out of place facing a firing squad, the judge made the rounds of the exhibits, crash helmet still firmly wedged beneath one arm. He looked each competitor straight in the eye, almost as if he was trying to remember a face. He paused at each tank, taking a curious look at each fish and making a note on his clipboard. He consulted the results of previous shows, looking for a name or a face. Knowing looks and worried frowns flew around the room. He came to an exhibit that seemed to hold his attention. A large silver angel fish stared languidly ahead, indifferent to his opinion. Its owner was a little less so. With the build of a wrestler and a face that would look more at home at an illegal boxing match than a timid tropical fish show, he met the judge's stare and a knowing smile creased the judge's face. The big man had the decency to blush and look away as the judge fingered a slight mark beneath his left eye, a fading reminder of their last encounter. With a flourish he marked a large X upon his sheet of paper. He continued on his rounds and I might have imagined it, but he seemed to have a bounce in his step now.

Soon the time to award the prizes came and all eyes fell upon the little judge. With his helmet now firmly strapped in place and what might have been a home-made gum shield in his mouth, though that could be just the way he smiles, he awarded his rosettes with a flourish. A heavy set woman with short hair and sensible shoes won first prize with a Tinfoil Barb that even I could see had a hint of fin rot. Second prize went to an eighty-year-old grandmother showing a below average Oscar and who only came to the shows for the company. Third prize went to a colourful Discus, not because it was a particularly good specimen of its breed, but because it happened to be the closest tank to the door. With that the judge was gone, a muffled giggle from his helmet and a hand gesture that could be charitably construed as a wave goodbye. The hushed silence soon gave way to protests and angry exchanges between competitors, with the general consensus that the judge had been born out of wedlock, had some unsavoury social habits and was unaccustomed to the basic tenets of hygiene. I took this as a good time to make my own exit, lest I was forced to take sides.

Back on the street and with the angry din fading behind me, I made my way back to my car. It still had four wheels, which was a relief, and I could detect no obvious signs of damage. Wary Asian eyes regarded me from across the street, our oriental friend had discovered that there's more than one kind of jungle. I was about to get into the car when I noticed the little judge, still in his crash helmet, standing at the corner. He approached me cautiously, trying to remember if I was friend or foe.

'Could you give me a lift back into the city?' he asked, and looked as if he was ready to run away if I answered in the negative.

'What about your motorbike?' I asked, feeling a little confused.

'Oh, I don't have a motorbike; I came out here on the bus.'

A knowing smile creased his face and just for a moment the hardness left his eyes. I saw him in a new light as the full picture became clear. A little respect was due.

'Taking care of some unfinished business, huh?'

'Something like that.'

'Sure, why not? Hop in.'

He looked around in all directions, deemed it safe to remove his helmet, and climbed into the front passenger seat. He produced a plastic bag from one of his many pockets and put the helmet inside. He sat back and stared straight ahead, grinning like an idiot. I made my way out of the estate, passing my two ten-year-old friends who were pushing a hand cart with some cinder blocks on the top. They didn't seem happy to see me, but I tooted the horn and waved cheerfully to them anyway. My mood seemed to be improving the further I got from the community centre, or maybe that idiot smile was just infectious. I never did learn the name of the intrepid judge, but as we neared the city I asked his advice on tropical fish. His reply; get a budgie!

THE STAIRWAY
Neil Wesson

In a tastefully furnished first floor room Henry Sullivan sat at a writing desk. He checked through a large ledger to see who would be calling on him that day. The clock on the mantelpiece was striking eleven o'clock as Sullivan looked out of the window at the bustling city below.

The first of today's business would be calling on him shortly. A single oil lamp illuminated the room, this was placed on the top of his desk. It burned to serve only one purpose, to aid with the reading of the assorted papers piled up neatly on the desk.

The only entrance to the room was a door situated at the top of a flight of stairs. The stairway was cold and unfurnished, no carpet lay on the floor, no banister rail protruded from the wall.

It was winter outside, but even in the balmy days of summer those who had the misfortune to tread the steps up to that room would feel a chill on the back of their neck. The fortunate ones would also have the experience on the return journey back down the stairs, just though the fortunate ones.

Outside the front door of the white stone property, times were hard in the city of Hull in the year 1885. Men returning from the Crimea, of which there were many, found it difficult to fit back into civilian life, jobs for the veteran soldiers were hard to come by.

The docks thrived with cargo coming and going from all parts of the world, the port was a vital link to the empire.

In the west of the city seagulls hovered above the fish docks waiting for a tasty morsel to come their way, while on the pier, box loads of fruit were being unpacked for the Humber Street Market.

As the dockers worked, the prostitutes watched from the doorways of the many pubs knowing that for many of the men, today was pay day, a busy night ensued.

A middle-aged woman, shabby in appearance stepped off the top flight of the staircase and stood outside Mr Sullivan's door. She paused outside the door, waiting a moment to compose herself. With a deep breath she knocked on the door.

For a moment nothing happened, then she felt something on the back of her neck, it was icy-cold. Drawing in a short, sharp breath she turned, but no one was there. The creak of the door opening took her attention back to the purpose of her visit.

'Come in Mrs Streetwater,' said Sullivan his body framed in the doorway.

The woman entered the room and stood in its centre. Sullivan closed the door behind her. As the catch clicked shut Mrs Streetwater shivered.

Sullivan eyed her from head to toe looking for any evidence of new garments on her person. It was clear to him that she possessed none. On every visit she had worn the same old filthy clothes. Sullivan sat at his desk and consulted his book, not that he had to, he knew the exact amount owing.

'You now owe fourteen shillings Mrs Streetwater, do you have this week's payment?' She said nothing. 'Well I'm waiting,' he sneered.

'No, Sir. I don't.'

'Well. What am I going to do with you?' Again she remained silent. She had heard the tales of his late payers, some were never seen again. 'Well?' he shouted at her.

'Sorry Sir, it was my youngest, Albert, I had to take him to the doctor's. His breathing was ...'

Sullivan interrupted her, 'I'm not interested in your petty domestic affairs,' he yelled, 'but I'm not a monster despite what some people say, you have until next week. Two weeks owing next week or I will not be so understanding.'

'Thank you Sir.' She turned towards the door.

Sullivan jumped out of his chair and opened it for her.

She passed through the door, her body as stiff and tense as a stone column, she was still afraid of what he could do to her before she made it out of the front door. He watched her closely as she passed him then slowly descended down the stairs. As she opened the front door onto the street she breathed again, then out of the corner of her eye she caught sight of something that made her run out of the house in blind terror.

At the bottom of the stairs there was an internal door. It had swung open and there standing in the kitchen was a dwarf of a man wearing a blood stained overall, while in his hand he carried a meat cleaver. A disfiguring scar ran down the left hand side of his face, from the forehead down over the eye stopping at the line of the jaw bone. He smiled at the woman's response, stepping out into the hall he closed the front door.

'Be ready, soon,' said his master's voice from the top of the stairs, 'I'll be the next one in, with a bit a luck.'

Accompanied by a laugh the dwarf disappeared back into the kitchen.

In the street outside the white stone house, a one armed man paused at the door. He took one last drag on his cigarette, flicked the stub into the road's central gutter before looking round. After that final turn of his head he opened the door and entered the house.

Slowly he climbed the stairway. Half-way up he felt a pressure building on his chest, cold engulfed him. He felt cold now and his legs wouldn't go another step upward, it was as though an invisible force was trying to stop him going any further.

Since he had returned from military service he had heard voices in his head, but never had he experienced something as strange as this.

'Go, go back,' said a voice deep inside his head. 'Heed my words, for I am Ian Foreman,' it continued.

The voices had started again, his head hurt, something inside his skull was beating like a hammer on anvil.

Composing himself he continued up the stairs and once at the top knocked on the door. With a creak the door opened. 'Mr Jackson, come in.' As the ex-army man passed through into the room his wake omitted a smell, which the nostrils of Sullivan picked up at once, though he didn't mention it, not yet. Slowly he returned to his seat and consulted his book, 'Now let me see.'

Ben Jackson looked at the floor as Sullivan read out his notes, 'You borrowed three guineas one month ago. This was to procure lodgings for yourself and 'tide' you over while you sort out employment, is that correct?' Silence was Jackson's only reply. 'Since then I have not seen a penny piece of my moneys in return. Do you have employment sir?' Again Jackson said nothing. 'Well?' Sullivan raised his voice.

'No, Sir. I have not, I have only had enough money to eat the smallest amounts of scraps.'

'Really. It would appear that you have enough sir to purchase smoking tobacco and matches. Is this a justified use for my money?'

'No Sir.'

'The loan is called in Sir, you will have the money to me by the end of the day.'

'That's impossible Sir, I need more time to find a ...'

'I have given plenty of time due to your being one of Her Majesty's men at arms. Normally I would take action after only one missed payment, you have had three sir, three.'

'I will try Sir, tonight, I will have it.'

'Very well,' agreed Sullivan.

'By the way,' Ben was pushing his luck, but for his own sake he had to know. He asked the question that to him seemed more important than the money owed, 'Who is Ian Foreman?'

'Foreman, what makes you ask that?' Sullivan asked.

'It was just a name that I heard.'

'He was a man who couldn't pay his debts,' Sullivan replied in an off-hand tone. He crossed over to the door and opened it for Jackson, 'Tonight, no later than six o'clock.'

As Jackson passed, Sullivan lifted up a walking stick from the stand next to the door. This particular stick was only used for special purposes as it was weighted with a lead insert. Raising it above his head to achieve maximum velocity he brought it down on the back of Jackson's neck.

Jackson lost consciousness as soon as the contact was made. His limp body rolled down the stairs landing at the bottom in a twisted heap. The interior door to the kitchen opened. There in the doorway, cleaver in hand stood the dwarf, an acidic smile on his face.

The smile turned to a look of determination as he brought the cleaver down shearing Jackson's head from his body.

'Clean that up, then make the usual arrangements,' Sullivan ordered the little man.

He returned to his office where he sat down at the desk and began to count the day's takings. The interest from his loans plus the trade with the local research hospital was reaping in quite a tidy sum. If his clients couldn't pay with money then the sale of their cadaver more than covered the amounts of the loan.

At six-thirty he had finished for the day. As he placed the pile of bills and coins into the safe he began to feel uneasy. A sense of being watched came over him, a rubbing sound was coming from the door to the stairs. Slowly he crossed the room as quickly as he could then opened the door. No one was there. It was dark now, he closed and locked the safe, then lit a candle. After extinguishing the gas lamp he set off down the stairway, the candle in his hand lighting the way.

Half-way down the stairs the flame blew out. This left him in almost total darkness. He took out the box of matches from his pocket and struck one of them. The flame was warm, he could feel the heat on his face, lighting the candle once more he took another step down the stairs, then stopped.

What he thought was approximately seven steps down at the bottom of the stairway he could see the figure of a man looking up at him. The flame from the candle was obscuring his view, so he moved it to one side.

'Who is it? Who's there?' he asked, but no one answered his call.

Each time he took a step down the figure moved down a step too. After four or five steps he realised that he should have been at the bottom of the stairway, but he wasn't. It went on. Turning to face upward back toward his office he no longer could see his office door, only stairs. Turning back to face the apparition he stared at the almost translucent figure.

'I know you,' he said walking down the stairs towards it. 'I know you, you're that no good Ian Foreman.' Then it dawned on him. Foreman had been one of his victims, Ian Foreman was dead, murdered by him and his cook.

The spectre smiled at Sullivan then slowly disappeared leaving him there. He ran down toward the front door, but it never came. On and on he went until he was out of breath.

He sat down on the stairs, his head in his hands, that candle beside him, the stairs with no end or beginning, no top or bottom.

BEDSIDE MANNERS
Anne Rolfe-Brooker

The Devil consulted his fireproof wristwatch. It was nearly noon and he had a lot to do with his day. An old gamekeeper was trying to renege on his bargain, and had fought off a legion of devils who had been despatched to carry him to Hell. Swearing and cursing, he had pulled the devils' tails, dented their heads with a spade, and blown holes in their stomachs with a sawn-off shotgun, and now the tattered army had returned to inform their master that they would sooner try to get into Heaven than be sent again to bring Old Sam back with them.

The only pragmatic conclusion to be drawn from their cowardly attitude was that he, the overlord of all the layers of Hell, would have to go and collect Old Sam's soul himself.

'Can't get the damned staff,' his infernal highness muttered to himself, as he transformed himself from a thick-skinned, red-eyed nightmare creature into a suave, sophisticated man-about-town character. 'Only think about themselves and to hell with anyone else.'

He was in a particularly unpleasant temper as his spies on Earth had reported that the latest government statistics showed a sharp increase in religious observance, which had made his shares in nuclear missiles and other multitudinous armaments plummet sharply.

He absent-mindedly smoothed the cuffs of his dress shirt, and checked the back pocket of his pinstripes to see if he had remembered to materialise a wallet - a must for a visit to humanity - and realised with something bordering on rage that he had forgotten to dematerialise his tail, which hung limply over his trousers' waistband. 'Hocum pocum be gone!' he said querulously, and the tail immediately disappeared, leaving a tall, dark, tailless man with black wavy hair, deep brown eyes, which had no compassion within them, and an otherwise youngish, handsome face. The Devil waved a languid hand, and muttered something under his breath, and there was a small flash, a strong smell of sulphur, and a noise like a motorbike backfiring.

The bang made Old Sam jump, which was rather unpleasant for him, as he was lying in bed with his head just under a mahogany cupboard, which held a multitude of useless objects collected in the course of he old gamekeeper's travels around the countryside.

The doctor had been, and had informed the patient that he had better prepare for the next world, but Old Sam was damned if he would, especially as if he did so, his soul was forfeit, owing to a rather foolish transaction is his youth with the Prince of Darkness. Now he saw that in front of him was not a legion of feisty little devils commanding, asking and then imploring him to go with them, but the boss man himself. 'Wondered when you'd get here,' Old Sam said bitterly.

The Devil smiled, displaying a set of extremely white, sharp teeth; enough to frighten off the most intrepid shark. 'Well, here I am, and there you are. And you have something of mine I think,' the Devil said conversationally, examining his fingernails while he spoke.

Old Sam snorted. 'Hmmph! I'm not going anywhere right now, and when I do, it won't be with you,' he said without a tremor in his voice.

The Devil advanced to the old man's bed, and sat companionably on it, looking down at the recalcitrant sinner. 'Now, now Sam, he said. 'Didn't I keep my end of the bargain? Didn't you inherit from your great uncle, which was what you said you wanted? Haven't you had a long and eventful life doing what you wanted to do and not what others wanted you to do, which was what you said you wanted? Didn't you marry the mayor's daughter, which was what you said you wanted to do? It's only fair that you make the payment you promised me.'

Old Sam laughed, but it did not have much humour in it. 'My great uncle was bankrupt, and I had to pay all the bills; your idea of an eventful life was evidently not the same as mine , and Cecilia Flithersmith turned out to be one of the naggiest women it has ever been my misfortune to meet, and the happiest day of my life was when I buried her!'

The Devil tutted. 'Dear, dear. We are bitter, aren't we? It can hardly be considered my fault if things didn't turn out as you expected. The fact of the matter is that you got what you asked for, and I am temporarily one soul down. Now breach of contract is not possible Sam, it just isn't possible. I therefore claim your soul.'

Sam struggled to rise in the bed and rested on one elbow, looking the Devil straight in the eye as he did so. 'Now you listen here, you misbegotten son of everything that's rotten - I am not going anywhere with you, and I am not prepared to part with my soul. You are in breach of contract, not me and if necessary I'll take you to court.'

The Devil laughed, and a bright flame shot from his nostrils as he did so, 'How absolutely priceless you are, you old goat! I know that lawyers will take on practically anything to make a fast fortune, but I can't think of anybody who believes enough in the Devil any more, to touch your case with a pitchfork. You have to remember,' he added confidentially, 'that with the loss of religion so recently rampant on this planet, belief in the Devil has disappeared along with the belief in God, thus making my job a lot easier. Now be a sensible man and prepare to leave.'

Old Sam smiled. 'You can't take me, you know. I've confessed and taken Communion, and repented fully.'

A look of disgust flickered across the face of the lord of the underworld. 'Your disgusting habits have nothing to do with the original bargain.' He flicked his fingers, and a piece of yellow parchment appeared in his hand. 'I have here,' he said confidentially, 'one agreement, signed by the party of the first part - that being you - to pay the party of the second part - that being me - one filthy, used, defiled soul at the end of a long and eventful life, subject to the fulfilling of two wishes, the one being the inheritance of your great uncle, (who unhappily and unbeknown to you, happened to be bankrupt), the other being the obtaining in marriage, the hand of one Cecilia Flithersmith, then spinster of this parish.'

Sam raised himself until he was eyeball to eyeball with the fiend. 'And I maintain that you knew my great uncle was bankrupt, and you knew Cecilia was the damnedest, devil-begotten bitch ever to cross a man's life.'

The Devil held the piece of parchment before the sick man's face. 'I do not know the paternity of your bride - I seriously doubt that she was devil-begotten, as I believe her mother was a religious bigot of awesome religiosity - but I strenuously deny that I knew any such thing about your nearest and dearest.' He pointed to the signature, Sam Sammes, and added, 'Even if I did, it does not affect the terms in any way whatever. You did not specify what you wanted to inherit from your great uncle, merely that you wanted to inherit, and you did not specify that your beloved was to be any way other than herself, which I believe was the case, and is now the basis of your objection to paying me, is it not?'

Old Sam pushed the parchment away with a gnarled hand. 'It is not an objection, old cock, it's a flat refusal. You've failed in your obligation to me, and I am claiming immunity under the Trades Description Act.'

Smoke began to pour from the Devil's nostrils now - he was getting really angry. Never in his whole existence had he come across such a cantankerous, argumentative and clearly dishonest old man. 'The Trades Description Act does not apply in Hell,' he said, 'and neither, before you mention it, does the European Court of Human Rights. Now stop being bothersome and prepare to accompany me to Hell!'

So saying, he rose from the bed, stood straight, and folded his arms, preparatory, it seemed, to muttering some incantation to transport the pair of them to their destination.

Old Sam crumpled the piece of parchment with one hand. 'I served 54 years of hell with Cecilia. She was a frigid, vindictive, gossip-mongering shrew of a woman, a hell-cat with nothing in her mind save the causing of pain, discomfort, humiliation, embarrassment and anger to all who crossed her path, and most notably to me. She had the tongue of a viper and the heart of a gorgon. She knew neither kindness nor compassion and her favourite pastime was goading, beating, berating and shackling me, in mind and body and spirit. Hell, you say? It sounds like paradise in comparison. The only problem is that she is undoubtedly already there waiting, like a cat for an injured mouse, for me to arrive and turn her perdition into something akin to Heaven.' With that, he sank back on the pillows, his eyes bright with undisguised fury.

The Devil looked pensive. 'Certainly she sounds like a candidate for us. I can't say that I have met the woman, but if she is as you say she is, I can't imagine how I've overlooked her. She sounds like everything I've ever dreamed of in a mean and malicious soul.' He clicked his fingers and a mobile phone appeared in his left hand. Dialling the number of the Beast, he waited for a few moments for an answer from one of his demons, tapping one cloven foot impatiently as he did so. 'Ah, hello Asmodeus,' he said at last, 'do we have any record of Cecilia Flithersmith on our files? Nasty piece of work, died about ...' He glanced at Old Sam, who held up four fingers - 'about four years ago, Earth time.'

Old Sam mouthed something at him, and the Devil paused. 'Cecilia Sammes,' Old Sam whispered, not Flithersmith.'

'Oh, of course,' the infernal being said. 'Hello? Scratch Flithersmith - it's Cecilia Sammes I want.' He waited a little while, his lips pursed in thought, until Asmodeus came back on the line. 'I see. Yes, well

Purgatory is certainly an alternative, although I think there has been a clerical error there somewhere. I am sure she should be one of ours. What have we got on the state of her soul?' He smiled in what he thought was a reassuring manner towards Old Sam, but the teeth were too sharp, too white, and the eyes too cold to convey anything but impending damnation. 'Yes, that's it. She's certainly one of ours. I am going to personally kick ass when I get back. I cannot stand the slipshod attitude the demons are displaying lately. The whole damned clerical system has gone to pot, and I shall want to know why.' He clicked off the mobile and sat on Sam's bed again. 'Well, I think I ought to thank you Sam, he said. 'There was an infernal error somewhere along the line, and you wife managed to slip into Purgatory. Only had another nine hundred years to go, and she'd have been home and dry.'

Sam waved one arm feebly in acknowledgement.

'Still, that leaves us with the problem of your payment,' the Devil said.

Old Sam closed his eyes and let out a sigh. 'Just get it over with,' he said resignedly. 'Just get on with it.'

The Devil clasped Sam's hand with ice-cold fingers. 'Well you can't complain really,' he said, 'everybody knows that a bargain with the devil has a sting in its tail. It is most unfortunate, even by my standards, that you got absolutely no pleasure out of the deal, and I do sympathise, as much as I am able, in that you will now have to spend eternity with your late unlamented wife, but if I were to make an exception in your case, you'd be amazed at the number of lost souls there would be, claiming it as a precedent, and that would never do, because we should have to implement divorce in Hell, making Heaven somewhat redundant. You see my problem?'

Old Sam nodded weakly and with a flash, a bang, and a strong smell of sulphur, Devil and Sam were spirited away to the land of waiting wives ...

INFORMATION

We hope you have enjoyed reading this book - and that you will continue to enjoy it in the coming years.

If you are interested in becoming a New Fiction author then drop us a line, or give us a call, and we'll send you a free information pack.

Alternatively if you would like to order further copies of this book or any of our other titles, then please give us a call or log onto our website at www.forwardpress.co.uk

New Fiction Information
Remus House
Coltsfoot Drive
Peterborough
PE2 9JX
(01733) 898101